BEYOND THE FILIGREE WALL

MELISSA WRIGHT

Cover design and illustration by Ireen Chau

Interior illustrations by

Ireen Chau https://www.ireenchau.com

EK Belsher http://www.ekbelsher.com

Victoria van Herckenrode @vicsdrawss

EmberMarke https://www.embermarke.com

Grace Crandall @krasnetigritsa

BEYOND THE FILIGREE WALL

PROLOGUE

The good king-fearing people of Westrende held a single faith without question: *magic isn't real*. Stories of fae were only constructs designed to explain away the sort of unpleasantness no one wished to examine over-much—unpleasantness like the madness that struck when the moon was full, when a maiden went lost, a child fell ill, or perhaps when a king's gold was stolen and the wheat stores turned foul. That sort.

Myth, superstition, and deception were what the tales were made of.

Etta, neither unreservedly good nor especially king-fearing, knew the truth was far simpler. Beneath their willful ignorance and outright denial rested a dark secret, depthless in its desire for vengeance. Indeed, the people of the kingdom had no notion that they were only a single misstep from plummeting over a deadly precipice. They liked it that way.

Lady Antonetta Ostwind, sole daughter and heir of the great General Ostwind, had kept that vile secret since she was a girl. *Tell no one*, her father had warned in whispered threats. Tell no one of the monsters who'd come for her mother while

1

Etta had watched from the darkness beneath her bed. *Speak of them, and they shall come again.* She had bitten down on the words until she tasted blood. She had not spoken, had not screamed, had not uttered a single word of the fae in all the days which followed.

It had not stopped their coming because the fae had been there all along.

Antonetta could see through their glamour. Her father's fear and the king's council may have kept Etta from shouting the truth, but it could not take her sight. The fae, magical beings intent on doing harm, walked among them. Lesser fae may have seemed harmless if not for the shadows—beings like those who had taken her mother, darker in both intent and form. Shadows, they were called, because to acknowledge the existence of the high fae of the Riven Court was to meet a disagreeable fate.

Etta had been forced into a secrecy meant to protect her, but it had protected only the monsters. She understood precisely the ruin they caused because she could see a truth at which no one else dared look. The fae were worse than any imagined tales. And her silence had kept them safe. Her hands had not spilled their blood.

All that was about to change.

CHAPTER 1

"Nearly there," Nickolas chirped. Blond, approaching five and twenty, and apparently entirely at ease being cramped inside a juddering cabin for days, Nickolas Brigham—Etta's escort, onetime childhood friend, and several-time nemesis—had been unashamedly vying for her attention for the entire trip.

Etta stared out the window of the carriage. There was nothing particularly outstanding beyond the cloudy glass, but there was equally nothing outstanding about her, and she wasn't fool enough to believe his attentions were genuine. Nickolas was tall and handsome and had the sort of crooked smile that made many a knee go weak. Though passable in many respects, Etta was little different than the other ladies at court, of which he surely had his pick. She understood full well that his attention—like nearly all attentions she'd been paid since she was young—came not from any special beauty or grace but from her standing.

As head of the council, Etta's father was the most influential of a dozen men and women who directed the fate of the kingdom and all those within it until a king was returned to power—which, at the rate things were going, would not be anytime soon. It was no secret that the current prospects were all a good decade short of meeting the age and education requirements to become king, and two of those prospects had recently been stricken ill.

Furthermore, in a matter of days, Etta herself would become marshal, head of law and order in the kingdom and responsible for overseeing the guard. She was not about to cock it up for a boy like Nickolas, who would get no further than captain without an advantageous marriage. She drew in a long breath, comforted by what was to come once she was finally installed into the office of marshal. The position was significant in that it alone allowed freedom of movement beyond the council. She'd be tied no longer to their foolish rules and society games. They would be unable to stop her from crossing the Rive.

"You must be excited to return after all these years," Nickolas said. "Eager? Relishing the tingle of anticipatory glee, perhaps?"

She continued her regard of the unkempt grass beyond the carriage window. The seemingly endless expanse of sky had been overcast most of the day and was beginning to color with a tinge of pink to herald the coming sunset. The trip had been planned in exacting detail to allow for the carriage's timely arrival—even if that arrival was two days prior to her father's expectations—because none were allowed to cross the border once night had fallen.

The kingdom gates, twisted dark iron topped with deadly barbs, tucked neatly between walls of the finest stone, came into view. A line of kingsmen stared down from the parapets, surely aware even from such a height who warranted the pomp of the approaching caravan. She would be scrutinized regardless. They would make her wait outside the gates while her documents were verified, even with Nickolas and his ilk at her side. She glanced back to the rest of her escort, kingsmen of varying status perched in full regalia atop prized horses. More than one of her protectors seemed to have an eye on the line of trees in the distance. Even Nickolas seemed a bit fidgety in the dying light.

It was telling that the people of Westrende denied the existence of fae and magic, yet not a soul seemed comfortable with a wait outside the gates so near where the dark forest loomed. As if the Rive might reach out and snatch them.

Etta scoffed. "Nickolas," she said, finally giving him her gaze. "Tell me what I have missed."

His smile was golden, a great, glowing, ridiculous thing that seemed to light up the carriage. By the wall, he had always been so mulishly oblivious. She wasn't certain he'd ever been able to read a person's mood—or maybe he'd simply not bothered to care if, in the end, doing so didn't further his cause. One more trait it seemed he'd not outgrown. She gestured for him to get on with it.

"Little has happened that was not relayed in your reports, I'm sure, my lady." His smile hinted that he in fact knew exactly what she was about—mood and all—and intended to toy with her.

She gave him her flattest expression.

His grin shifted into something a bit more tenable. "Lady Yates is having a torrid affair with a barber's son. Theo's carpenter was caught using funds meant for suite furnishings to procure an absolutely obscene collection of crystal urns, which were discovered by a maid while freshening the mattresses." He waved a hand vaguely near the curtain, as if drawing the memories from air. "A pair of scribes was caught desecrating the king's garderobe, and the magistrate had them pilloried in their small-clothes for a week."

She managed not to wince. Castle gossip wasn't at all something she'd missed about being away, and certainly not the information she'd been after from Nickolas. "What of the new chancellor?"

The answering spark in his eyes teased something that Etta did not like at all. He leaned forward on the seat, his long fingers woven together only inches from her knee, the scent of roses and sandalwood wafting off him. "Ah, yes," he said. "Gideon."

Gideon. He was going to be hideous. She could tell already. "Yes."

"Nephew to our great steward."

Etta had never met the new chancellor but had heard well enough: he was a brutal tactician with no regard for new ideas, no interest in improvement to their ancient laws and inter-kingdom protocol, and not a whit of tolerance for those who crossed the wall. "He's a traditionalist," she said.

Nickolas chuckled. "You could say that."

"I did. What would *you* say?"

He leaned back, tossing his hands a bit before sliding them over the slick blue fabric that covered his knees. "I'd call him a raging cumberground. An absolute saddle-goose. Ineffective as a boat full of holes." He shrugged. "But that's just me."

Well, now he was just trying to buy her with flattery. Etta nodded. "We shall see."

The man had been installed after she'd gone away—been sent away—for her training. In the nearly four years since, he'd risen to the head of chancery with unlikely speed. It was a position that rivaled hers. There was every expectation he would become the marshal's mortal enemy.

Etta intended to crush him.

AFTER THEY HAD BEEN PERMITTED through the gates and winded their way through the kingdom under a sky that had turned turbulent, the carriage, at long last, drew to a stop before their destination. Said destination was not the front entrance of the castle to a grand reception, as would surely have been planned by her father's staff. Etta had demanded that Nickolas both keep their arrival confidential and deliver her to the service entrance. She needed to prepare for her reintroduction to the council and courtiers on her own terms, and in time to suss out what else they might have planned for her. Besides, she wanted greatly to wash the days of travel from her person before meeting a single soul.

Shoving a lock of her chestnut hair behind an ear and sorting her disheveled skirt into order, she drew a fortifying breath of stuffy cabin air.

When she glanced up, Nickolas was watching her, a sly grin on his stupid charming mouth. "Ready, my lady?"

She would not reward him with a glare, never mind that his tone had been loaded. They both knew she was walking blindly into a lion's den, against the general's orders. "Nickolas," she said, "I am always—"

His bark of laughter broke the stillness she only then realized had come over them. He placed a hand over his heart and slid forward in his seat. "Yes, it is not as if you have ever let me forget." The door opened, and his long legs carried him past her in one graceful motion to land outside the carriage and between a waiting pair of umbrella-wielding ushers. He leaned in and adopted a conspiratorial tone. "The lady Ostwind is always ready."

Despite the dread that sank in her belly, Etta took his proffered hand. "Yes," she said. "Always."

Etta was not ready. A single flash of her reflection in the ornate metal trim that lined the carriage door made her state painfully clear. She stepped out regardless, just as the murky sky let loose and poured rain onto the fine cobbled drive.

Nickolas glanced at the deluge, taking hold of one umbrella while leaving the second for the ushers. "Portentous."

She resisted the urge to jab an elbow into his ribs. The space between the carriage and the entrance was excessive and scattered with mounted kingsmen eager to return their charge. Until the general's daughter was safely inside, their duty was not complete. Etta took hold of the umbrella with Nickolas, and they weaved swiftly between the beasts with their clattering hooves and the castle staff converging on the carriage to retrieve the pair's many trunks.

Beneath the overhang at the entrance, Etta stopped to shake the umbrella and draw another breath. Her apprehension was nearly under control when a black dog shot from beyond a column to dart past her skirts. She shrieked—an absolute embarrassment she would dwell on when she wasn't thusly occupied—leaping back into Nickolas, who brushed off the arms of his embroidered suitcoat.

Clearly not expecting the collision, he barely caught her before they both tumbled to sprawl on the rain-soaked cobblestone. As it was, his boot splashed into an impossibly fast-forming puddle, splattering wet filth up the leg of his fine trousers and half of Etta's skirt. She did not bother with explanation or apology because in that moment, she became aware that the creature had been no dog at all.

It had been a lesser fae. Etta said a curse, gritted her teeth, and took tighter hold of the closed umbrella. Stomping through the door on its trail, she dodged two serving men and a downstairs maid before she caught sight of the dark mass of fur sliding around a corner. She was after it without another thought.

Etta had made a promise to herself while she'd been away:

not a single fae would pass her sight without coming to regret it. Her silence was over. They would pay for what they had done.

The thing darted into a storeroom, turning to give her a savage grin made of too many teeth before the door slammed closed behind it. Etta picked up her pace, shoving through after it, rain-soaked weapon in hand. The door snicked shut behind her, throwing the narrow room into near darkness. The creature had disappeared, but she could feel its eyes upon her and almost sense the horrid glee vibrating through it.

A drop of rain fell from her umbrella to splat loudly on the pantry floor. In the shadows, something giggled.

"Come out, you filthy—"

A solid slab of wood smacked into Etta from behind, Nickolas and the light of the main room coming along with it. The creature shot across the space, and Etta took an off-balance swing just as Nickolas grabbed her in some dramatic and entirely misplaced heroic gesture that she made a note to discuss with him at a later date. The swing missed, the umbrella thwacked into a sack of flour, and Etta was quite suddenly covered in a matted, pale paste. The creature shoved her to land face-first into the sack then darted out the open door.

Etta lay there for a moment, swallowing words she'd sworn she would never eat again. A lock of hair was wedged into her mouth. Her knee throbbed. And the beast must have gotten a swipe in on its way through because she felt the thin stinging line of the cuts she'd grown accustomed to as a girl. Several cuts, it seemed, began to burn near her ankle.

"By the wall," Nickolas murmured, staring down at the mess in apparent awe.

"The wall indeed," she said through gritted teeth then flopped to her back so she could glare up at him.

They came out of the storeroom to an audience of at least a dozen kingsmen and castle staff. Etta slapped a hand to her skirt, which puffed what flour had not yet caked on, then threw the umbrella to the floor. "Ladies, gentlemen, so good to see you once more." Then she tottered off on flour-caked heels without a single look back.

Nickolas found her in the first empty corridor she'd come to, pounding her fists on the wall with a curse entirely unseemly for one of her station.

"Etta," he said, his voice low, careful, and not at all in a tone he'd used in their many days of travel.

"No. Don't. Just—I need to return to my rooms."

"Absolutely," he answered with not a single question about why she had just attempted murder on a rangy dog. "Only"— he glanced over his shoulder—"let me be certain word of this doesn't leave the, uh..."

Etta groaned.

"Right," he said. "One moment."

She turned to lean against the wall of the empty corridor, jerked her wet gloves off, and threw them to the floor. The narrow passage was used by staff, poorly lit, sparsely decorated, and unlikely to be occupied at the current hour. Not that it mattered. She'd been planning her triumphant return to Westrende since the day she was shipped off to school. And there she was, all her care and caution exhausted within minutes of her arrival.

She unbuttoned her lace-trimmed jacket and yanked her arms free of the damp material, tearing seams by the sound of it. It went in a pile with her gloves. Bending over to ruck up her skirts, she cursed again when she saw the damage the thing had done to her leg. "This is why I hate dogs," she muttered, as if in reply to all the remembered comments she'd been unable to answer to honestly since she was a girl. "Cannot trust a single one not to be fae."

She snapped the skirt down and wrapped her arms around her middle, wondering if she might succeed in navigating to her rooms without Nickolas there to clear a path. By the sight of her, it was probably best she didn't try. She sighed, closed her eyes, and leaned back against the wood-paneled wall.

Door, her mind corrected just as it fell open behind her. She fell with it. Her arms went out, scrabbling for purchase, and caught only one side of the frame. She felt more than heard the intake of breath of the person she'd pitched into and drew herself up to turn and look. It was a dark-haired man in his early twenties, impossibly near. His square jaw had gone slack in an improbably perfect face, everything else about him entirely buttoned up. He wore a high-collared black shirt beneath a well-fitted black suit, not a lick of fanciful trim upon him. Against his chest was clutched a sleeve of parchment, his long fingers curling more posses- sively around it as she watched.

Then her eyes rose to his, dark beneath thick lashes and soft with something akin to bewilderment. That was when she remembered, quite suddenly, that half her clothes were strewn across the floor.

"Oh," she said, searching for anything at all she might say to the poor man. She drew herself up. "Lord—" She stopped and cleared her throat, unsure of his identity. He seemed vaguely familiar, but she had been gone for four years. People changed.

"Lord Alex—" he started almost automatically then abruptly cut himself off to stare back at her. He did not appear to have the same sort of trouble with recognition Etta was experiencing. His tone changed. "What precisely are you about?"

Her mouth came open without a single answer in mind just as Nickolas burst back into the hallway, announcing, "Done, we're covered. Saved you from a spanking no doubt

—" His words fell off, his wink and stride stuttering to an awkward halt as he took in the scene.

He decidedly did not look down at Etta's clothes on the floor or her person, which gained him a point in her tally, but neither did he explain what they were about, which, to be fair, seemed unlikely to be believable in any case. He cleared his throat, not unlike what Etta had just done.

The new arrival glanced between them, apparently making his own assumptions. "This behavior is entirely unseemly for persons of your station."

Nickolas ran a hand over his chest, seeming to fight a smile. "Quite." He stepped forward, resuming his casual posture as he approached the pair. He held an arm toward Etta. "My lady. Perhaps we shall take this kind advice in the spirit it was given and remove ourselves to your rooms."

Etta's gaze darted between Nickolas and the other man. She felt her cheeks heat, but she was not sure precisely where to direct her ire, had she even the energy to unleash it. She decided she didn't have to. She was an Ostwind. Without a word in farewell, she bent to pick up her things then turned and strode away, Nickolas's chuckle echoing behind her.

CHAPTER 2

Etta stopped at the door to her rooms, a sense of familiarity twisting in her gut. Her hand was frozen, unable to touch the lever that would let her inside. Angry at herself for being incapable, she turned her back and leaned on the finely carved wood to shoot a look at Nickolas. "This has been a disaster."

He grinned. "Entirely." He handed over a flour-caked glove she'd apparently missed in her hasty escape. "And it's barely begun."

The dread in her stomach turned to lead. He was right. She still had to face her father and the council, never mind that she'd not yet conquered her childhood rooms. "Well," she managed, her tone making clear she would not be inviting him inside. "I suppose you've some advice for me in that matter?"

His bright eyes stayed on her a moment too long then flicked briefly to her mess of attire. "No, I think you have it well in hand. May luck be in your favor, my lady." Nickolas inclined his head toward her in something of a bow then turned to go, merrily twirling a ribbon that she was fairly certain had been attached to her gown not a quarter hour before.

Etta let her head drop back to the door. It hit with a rather solid *thunk,* and she sighed. When she finally went inside her room, the hopelessness only became worse.

Drapes rested over the furniture—her room disused in the years she'd been gone. Had she returned when she was meant to, the space would have been set to rights, its decorations polished and shined, windows opened, tapestries beaten, the tables topped with generous bouquets. She had not returned when she was meant to, and not solely because she was a coward.

Etta had been tired of waiting, tired of pretending all was well. She'd been eager to come home because she'd been afraid that if she didn't come back on her own, her father might take his chance to stop her.

In the darkness, she ran a hand over the drape that covered a side table, her fingers brushing the carved trim through the fabric as it caught on a familiar nicked edge. It didn't matter that the furniture was hidden. The memories remained. She did not search for candles. She had no tinder. Across the sitting room, she opened one side of the double doors to her bed chamber. The room was dim, lit only by the occasional flicker of far-off lightning through the windows and what moonlight made it past the storm. Rain pattered against the glass in waves.

Do not speak of them. Tell no one.

Speak of them, and they will come again.

There, by the narrow door that led to her closet, they had wrapped their hands around her mother's arms. And there, where sunlight would make a pattern of squares on the fine wood floor come morning, she had dropped her dagger. Etta moved forward, her feet silent and her breathing slow. There, beneath the bed, Etta had waited, watching it all without a word.

Lightning flashed in the same moment when something moved in the room behind her. Etta spun, hand to her side, but here in Westrende, she wore no sword. Weapons were for the training yard, for uniform dress. Etta had been relegated to a mere lady home from school, traveling beneath the protection of her father's guard. Just because she'd learned how to use a weapon didn't mean her father would allow her to wield it in his domain.

"My lady." The maid carried one end of a trunk and gave a little curtsy, tugging the burden and, in turn, the arms of the footman on the other end. "Sorry to have startled you. The storm must have drowned out the sound of my knock."

Etta waved the apology away as two more footmen came inside. They moved through the space in a practiced flurry, efficiently removing the furniture drapes and lighting candelabra.

"A shame we were not warned ahead of time," the maid remarked as she started opening Etta's trunks. "We could have had your rooms ready if we'd known."

"Please." Etta leaned down to stay the woman with a gentle hand on her arm. "I'll have a fire and water for a bath, but the rest I can do on my own."

The woman gave her a narrow-eyed look but made no comment on the state of Etta's wardrobe. "Very well. But be warned, we'll be in for a full cleaning tomorrow." She snapped her fingers at the footmen. "You heard the lady. Send up Greta with water and have someone from the kitchens bring a nice dinner. The lady looks as if she could do with some local fare." She shifted, facing Etta full on. "You'll remember where the bell pull is, my lady."

Etta smiled. "I believe so, yes."

She nodded. "Very well, then. Good to have you back."

At the maid's command, the pack of footmen exited the room in an order that would have made any general proud. Etta stared down at the row of trunks in the warm light of the candelabra, not particularly eager for the task of unpacking. With any luck, a hot bath would ease her stiffness from the days of travel.

When she heard the door open once more, she assumed it must have been Greta with her water. She glanced absently toward the entrance, her heart catching in her throat at the sight of the figure in the doorway. *Not the maid.*

"How dare you?" Her father's words were low and even, but Etta felt them like a slap. Her mouth snapped shut, her expression level as she straightened to face him in the manner he'd always expected—the manner that had been drilled into her further during the past four years of training.

He closed the door then crossed the space in a few brisk strides. Standing before her, he was as imposing as ever, despite that Etta had grown in the years she'd been gone. It was difficult not to flinch, but she stood tall, shoulders back and bearing proper.

"Do you have no care for the risk you have taken? No concern for how your disobedience casts shame on the Ostwind name? You have not only defied a direct order but blackened the reputations of a dozen trained men. It is not you alone who will pay for your transgressions."

Etta drew a sharp breath. "You cannot punish those men. They acted under my orders. They've done nothing at all but—"

His response was swift and forceful. "I cannot? I cannot, you tell me. Here in the domain of the kings of Westrende, under the protection of the king's army, an unbanded girl tells the commander of it all what he may or may not do."

"Father, I—"

"Father, is it? Not General now, not when it is convenient for you to forget my responsibilities to council and kingdom?"

She swallowed hard. She had known he would not be pleased when she'd subverted his plans, but she hadn't intended to bring punishment upon the kingsmen who had helped her. "I didn't think," she said sullenly. She could not say the truth, could not admit that she'd felt as if she had no other choice. "The blame rests solely on my shoulders."

"Your shoulders." He shook his head, as if she'd not heard a word he'd said. "I had hoped that the years away would have helped you grow out of reckless actions and impudent notions. I see that it has not."

"You shipped me off for four years, as if I mattered not at all. Three kingdoms away, as far as you could manage."

His voice was ice. "I would send you off for another four if I could."

Etta felt herself blanch. Her insides twisted into a tortuous knot. He had confirmed all her fears in a single blow. Then something else rose in her, wild and hot. "Reckless, you say. Impudent." She leaned forward, almost daring him to act. "I watched them take her from this very room—"

General Ostwind was a formidable man. Etta understood that. He commanded armies, was head of the council that, as he was so fond of reminding her, ran the kingdom. But the speed in which he closed the distance, palm slipping over her mouth in a move that might prove deadly with a different motive, stunned her. Her arms dropped limply at her sides, her heart beating like a rabbit's.

She stared at him with wide eyes. Short, sharp breaths puffed through her nose where it brushed the side of his hand.

He did not let go of her. "I forbade you to speak of them."

Etta was very still for a very long moment. When he did not let go, she nodded beneath his grip.

Her father watched her, possibly considering punishments, possibly making certain she understood him clearly. Etta might never know.

When he spoke, it was in a cold whisper. "Your mother was taken for the same foolish impudence. Remember that when you invoke her memory." The warning settled in the bare space between them, slow and tumbling like a stone through water. It would remain there forever, Etta knew, piled upon its brethren, too far beneath the surface to ever pluck free.

Finally, he stepped back. "Council is meeting at cockcrow. You will attend. Homecoming celebrations will be canceled. Your work begins now."

She swallowed, unable to quite form a response.

He turned without another word, but when he reached the door, he looked back. "If I hear a single utterance more of this nonsense, you will be removed from consideration for the post of marshal. Indeed, from any post at all."

The door shut behind him like a punch to her midsection.

ETTA HAD LIVED with strangers in a distant kingdom for four long years, waiting for her return with the constant fear that it might never happen, that she'd been sent away to be dealt with—and not as a true threat, but merely an inconvenience. *That cannot be his purpose,* she'd told herself. *It is nothing so nefarious as that.* She had been lying to herself. Removing Etta from Westrende and its fae with the greatest distance possible had been no accident.

There was no room for taking chances. Etta needed to secure her spot as marshal, the only thing that might gain her solid footing. The meeting with council was paramount. And she was running late.

Her feet moved silently through the corridor, her lips running with wordless curses for the nightmares that had kept her awake. She'd dressed in a trim gown and coiled her hair hastily at the nape of her neck. A splash of cold water was all the attention she'd paid her face before blotting it dry, the dark rings beneath her eyes unheeded.

She had no time to spare, but when her steps faltered, it was of their own accord. In the long corridor outside the council chamber, an endless row of paintings was strung high on either wall.

Her mother's portrait was among them. Her father's, too, but Etta had seen him in the flesh. In the darkness of her room at school, Etta had longed to stand so close to the familiar strokes of color, the soft curve of amber hair, the warm plane of cheek that met a small crescent of shadow near her mother's deep rosy lips, an ever-present hint of humor that even the artist could not bear to hide. The entire corridor was lined with paintings of Westrende officials, a tribute to agents of the kingdom.

Etta's would be installed next. Before she took her position, she would be painted in the fine uniform of marshal, the highest level of law enforcement in Westrende, and given the band that marked her as an agent of the kingdom. Etta would head the branch of law that, unlike chancellor or magistrate, would be allowed free rein beyond the castle walls. Freedom to move through the entire kingdom would be hers.

In a matter of days, she would be appointed to the post, and her portrait would be hung in the same hallowed hall as her mother's in a ceremony for all the courtiers to see. Etta's father would be unable to remove her from the post or to force her from the kingdom ever again.

The sound of a gavel echoed from beyond the chamber

doors down the corridor. It was the call to order. She cursed, breaking into a sprint that had her winded by the time she reached the entrance. She took one steadying breath, swiped back a loose lock of hair, then strode into the chamber.

Every set of eyes in the room turned toward her. *Steady*, she reminded herself. Her victory was assured. The previous marshal was set to retire, and no one else had vied for the position with an Ostwind trained and ready. Whatever else her father had done, sending her away for her studies had ensured she would be prepared. It had guaranteed the spot was hers.

"Lady Ostwind."

Etta found Louis, owner of the voice that had greeted her and a man she'd known since she was a child, and gave him a friendly nod. He gestured toward the side of the room. "Session has just begun. Please take a seat."

If color rose to her cheeks, at least her expression remained calm and pleasant as she made her way past the half dozen kingdom officials on her side of the table. She took a seat in one of the many chairs lining the wall, great carved wooden things with embroidered cushions and a poor view of the table's proceedings. If nothing else, it gave her time to survey the crowd.

Her father stood at the head of the table, a long, wide monstrosity that held permanent stations for the twelve members of the king's council. The council members' positions were permanent as well. Over half of the members were silver-haired, and two had been doddering along even before Etta had gone away. It did not mean their minds were not sharp, however. Each held impressive skill of both wit and weapon. At three and sixty, Louis still wielded a sword as well as any younger man, and the lady Cerys had deadly aim with a dagger despite that she was barely able to see across a room.

A clerk and two scribes sat further down the same row of

chairs as Etta, and several more figures watched from seats near the opposite wall. She was blocked from seeing precisely who the others were, as the lady Maura's assistant stood at his mistress's side, passing ledgers and notes as they were requested and obstructing a decent view.

For nearly two hours, the council heard reports from each bough of the absent king's rule, arguing over much of it then pushing proposed changes off until another meeting. Nothing had changed. She supposed she should have expected no less. They moved on to petitions, and as each was processed or set aside, the attendants around Etta thinned to none. Her father stood once more, as if to dismiss the meeting, and Etta was on her feet before she could stop herself.

"Yes." He frowned. "One more item to address before we withdraw."

Etta moved nearer the table at the end opposite her father, where no chair blocked her from view of the dozen members. She gave each one her gaze, direct and proper. Despite how much a girl her father made her feel, Etta was ready to take on the post.

"Ah, yes. The lady Ostwind is to be nominated for marshal." Stefan—warm eyes, warm complexion, cool disposition—watched her for a moment before his brow drew down. "I believe this was on next week's agenda. Come back early, have you?"

The general gave Etta a hard look. "Indeed. You all know the candidate's capacity. She has returned as primed as any candidate before her." His words were not spoken with the glowing pride one might expect. In fact, his tone was rather lacking in enthusiasm.

Shoulders back, Etta addressed the council. "As the general says, it's as if I've been trained in conflict since I could toddle." The chuckle that ran through the onlookers was gratifying, but she kept on. "I have met all requirements, including age, education, and military training. My studies since childhood have focused at length on law and history. I am prepared and well able to fulfill the duties of my post."

"Agreed," Maura said. "I see no reason to rake the coals with Lady Ostwind. I move that we bring the matter straight to vote."

"Seconded." Louis glanced down the table, apparently deciding the nays would be the easier vote to count. "Any opposed?"

There was a moment of silence in which Etta's heart swelled to the very walls of her chest. Not a single concern had been brought against her. It was no small thing—the office of marshal held considerable weight, and she'd only proven herself in her studies and in the training yard, not by working through the lower ranks. Her sacrifices had paid off. The years of brutal toil were about to be paid back in manifold abundance. She watched with deep pride as Cerys raised the gavel.

"Hold."

The voice came from the far wall of the chamber, an unsteady echo that shattered Etta's swollen heart. She stared, jaw slack, as Cerys's hand lowered the gavel to its side and a quiet rest.

Etta's eyes slid slowly from the gavel, past her watching father, to the wall from which the voice had come. A throat cleared, then a figure rose to stand tall in a long black robe, arms crossed before his waist. Recognition came immediately, as Etta had stared at the same face in the empty corridor only the night before. He looked slightly different, though he still wore the familiar disapproving frown. She suspected the difference was the robe of his office and, she saw now, that he wore the band that marked him not as some scribe or cleric, but an officer of Westrende.

A long silence followed, during which the man said

nothing more, his gaze on Etta. One of the council members shifted, and Etta realized her expression was not what one might consider polite. She smoothed it out as Louis spoke to the man. "You have something to add?"

He stepped forward, his attention on Etta. "I—" Abruptly, he looked to Louis. "Perhaps we should discuss it privately."

Louis's fingers flicked irritably against the parchment beneath his hand. "This is a council matter. Surely, it is not that she's the general's daughter, not in a kingdom that's been known to install a king's heir even as master of coin. It cannot be her age, not with you only a season or two older. Whatever your concern, out with it."

"I understand," the man said. "It is just that it's of a... more delicate matter."

Etta stiffened, as did several other council members. A pall fell over the room. "Speak up if you've seen something untoward. And do it now." Louis's tone felt like a warning.

The man seemed to take a steadying breath. "I have, in fact, witnessed behaviors most inappropriate from Antonetta Ostwind. I believe it incautious to allow her appointment."

The words hit Etta like the war hammers they'd used in training, swift and heavy and as if they meant to knock her to the ground. "What?"

General Ostwind stared on, his expression grim.

The man asked, "Do you deny only yesternight acting in a manner unbecoming of a person of your station, let alone the post to which you aspire?"

An outraged gasp tore from Etta, not particularly suiting the demeanor she was trying to present. There was nothing for it. She leaned forward. "I have done nothing of the—"

A telling stillness followed as Etta recalled what the man had seen. Etta, wet through and coated in flour, her jacket and gloves, and—oh yes—everything down to her bodice tossed in a pile on the floor. And Nickolas sauntering toward her, saying... *what had he said?* Right, that he'd saved her from a spanking. By the wall, there was no talking her way out of that one. Not in front of the council and her father. She wet her lips.

The look the general gave her was pure disappointment but not a hint of surprise.

Etta's jaw went tight, even as her dreams were crushed by a studious man in a drab robe. "You know nothing of the situation," she told him. "Why would you even consider this your concern?"

He stared at her, somber, staid, and a little as if she'd said something nonsensical. "Because I am chancellor. My very duty relies upon a marshal who is above reproach."

Her chest felt as if it had caved in, as if that swollen, shattered heart had fallen to her gut and taken with it the air that she might breathe.

Lord Alexander. Etta suddenly recalled the man starting to say the words, just before he'd given her a stern reproof about cavorting in the hallways. *Gideon. Alexander.* The single man who might bring her difficulties in her post.

She was going to murder Nickolas Brigham with her bare hands.

CHAPTER 3

"**A**ntonetta, do you dispute Lord Alexander's testimony?"

Etta bit back the "yes" that tried to leap from her tongue at Louis's question. Disputing the word of an official of Westrende was all but a criminal act. She'd not been installed in her post—she was still a citizen—and it would not be her word against his. It would be her word against the kingdom's. She wet her lips. "Not his testimony, only that it does not take into account the circumstances surrounding my actions."

Gideon Alexander stared at her. She could not precisely argue the details of the matter, so she gave her attention to the council instead. "Will none of you speak for me? You know well that my reputation has been above reproach." Even if she'd been gone for four long years, they had known her since she was a child.

"And yet, here is your reputation under reproach."

Louis's mouth had moved into a hard line. Emotion swelled hotly in Etta's throat. *Please*, she wanted to beg. *Please, don't do this.*

"Gideon," Cerys began, "do you care to elaborate on your concern?"

"I prefer not."

"Very well." She sighed. "It seems a great waste to allow the years Lady Ostwind has put toward service to the kingdom to no use. And yet, we cannot in good conscience allow a potential weakness in our defenses, given the importance of this post." Her cloudy eyes shifted toward the head of the table. "I propose a probationary period, during which Lady Ostwind will be under the watch of our chancellor. If she can perform to his satisfaction the duties his office assigns her, we will bring the nomination to vote once more. If not, then other candidates will be considered for the position. Say, by the next moon?"

A chorus of murmurs rose along with nods of approval around the council table as Etta's vision swam. Gideon had gone a shade paler. The general's lips turned down in displeasure. "Seconded," said someone at the far end of the table. Not a word rose in dissent when the vote was called.

"The ruling stands." Cerys's voice echoed through the chamber, followed by the terminal bang of gavel striking block.

Etta stared dumbly as figures moved around her to gather documents, break off into small discussions, or quit the room. One discussion in particular seemed more intense than the rest. Lord Alexander had cornered Cerys and Louis—seeing how quickly he might toss her from candidacy, no doubt, or trying to duck out of the second chance they'd offered her. She went for him, her feet moving without conscious thought, but Maura's assistant backed into Etta's path, landing a presumably unintentional elbow against her midsection. The assistant made a sound of surprise, fumbled his stack of documents, and caught them only by coming directly into her path. Another council member made to help the assistant, and by the time Etta found her way past the commotion, Gideon's drab robe was disappearing through the chamber door.

Etta rushed into the corridor, jaw clenched. The space was filled with loitering courtiers hoping to win a moment of the council members' time. She caught sight of her prey again just as he turned the corner into another corridor. It was a lesser used passage, a bit narrow and dark, but no one blocked her way, and she reached him before he made it to the final exit. He moved as if unaware of her presence, so she seized hold of his sleeve.

Gideon stopped abruptly, and Etta's momentum brought her a step too near. He seemed somehow taller as he stared down at her, his expression conveying nothing more than being taken aback. There was a moment of recognition after the instant of softness, then his gaze lowered deliberately to her grip on his arm.

She snatched her hand away, but her fingers curled into a fist at her side. She leaned toward him, keeping her voice low. "How dare you—"

"Lady Ostwind." His tone was detached, only serving to illustrate how out of control she'd become.

Reckless, her father had said. *Impudent.*

"How dare you," she started again. He only blinked at her, and her rage heightened to dangerous levels. She might actually have pummeled him with her fists. "Incautious? You're not certain? You do not even *know* me."

She all but spat the words, and something in his expression drew back as his shoulders suddenly became more square. He was no longer the meek clerk she'd nearly collided with the night before. He was no clerk at all—he was chancellor—and his bearing was that of a formidable man. In the dim light, he was all hard lines and shadows, a man who not only outranked her but outweighed her by half. "Were you not in a state of semi undress in a public corridor of this very castle only hours ago?" He did not need to add "with a known rakehell"—it was implied by his tone.

Her mouth snapped shut. She couldn't explain that she'd been chasing fae, not if she wanted to ever hold a position in the kingdom. That was the very point—no one else would believe. No one else would fight to keep them away.

"And have you not proven by your actions this very instant that you are incapable of the composure required to perform the duty you so zealously pursue?"

"Zealous? I have worked for this since I was no more than a girl. I have held my tongue against my father's expectations, against this council's rules, and against every slight ever paid me. All so I might one day—this day—*today*—finally be able to set right their ridiculous laws."

His brows lowered. "Do you hear yourself? You stand before a chancellor of Westrende and declare our laws absurd." He seemed to shake himself. When he took a step back from her, it became painfully clear how close they'd been standing—or rather, how far she'd come into his space. "Lady Ostwind, I intend to do everything in my power to prevent your nomination from returning to vote. It would be a dereliction of my duty to do otherwise."

Etta had been waiting her entire life to be free—free from her father, from the secrets, and free to seek justice for her mother. She opened her mouth, either to find a way to explain that to the man before her or to make a vow of her own—she hadn't decided which—when the sound of a throat clearing brought her up short.

"Lady Ostwind?" One of her father's assistants stood halfway down the corridor, looking concerned. The worry wasn't for her, she knew, but rather that if he'd been sent to find her, as with any task named by the general, he had better do it quickly. "I'm afraid your appointment still stands."

"Appointment?"

He inclined his head. "The portrait. Your father had us arrange the artist last night when the homecoming celebrations were being canceled. I realize that now, it may be unnecessary—"

"It is not unnecessary," Etta snapped. "Do not postpone it. I'll be just a moment."

She would be marshal by the next moon, by whatever means required. That was her vow and what she would tell Gideon Alexander. But when she turned back, Gideon was already gone.

CHAPTER 4

Nickolas was waiting for her in the connecting corridor, leaning casually against the wall in a long blue jacket. The rose in his hand was as bright as the golden embroidery on his vest. When she came into view, he straightened, smiling as if she'd accomplished something grand and twirling the rose stem between his fingers as if he was not a man about to meet his death.

His smile fell as she came to a stop mere inches before him. "The moment we are out of earshot of the council members in the next corridor, I am going to rip out the best of your entrails and feed them to Narine's raptors until the next moon."

He made a face. "The bird lady? You know I'm terrified of her."

"Precisely."

His nose scrunched. "Is this because of the Gideon thing?"

"The Gideon *thing*?" She stepped nearer, dangerously close to grabbing him by the lapels and shaking him like a rag doll. "You made an absolute fool of me."

Nickolas only pursed his lips as if biting down a smile, and Etta had to turn and leave to avoid attacking the man in the hall and making her situation even worse.

He rushed to catch up with her, tossing the rose into a tall urn near the wall. "Etta, please. It can't have been that bad. You excel under pressure. Always ready and all that."

"You're right," she said. "You didn't make a fool of me at all. I made a fool of myself." She glared sidelong at him. "He says I'm unfit to be elevated to marshal because of cavorting in the hallways with you. They refused to hold the vote."

Nickolas's step faltered, but when Etta kept on, he took a longer stride to reach her. "No."

"Yes. If I don't perform what I'm certain will be an impossible task, my chances of being anything—ever—are out."

To his credit, Nickolas looked as if he might be ill. It was all that saved him from a fist to the gut. "I thought it would be funny, that's all. I knew he was an ass, but I didn't think he'd actually contest your appointment. Did your father not stake his name for you?"

"No! He's furious that I've come back."

Nickolas frowned. "Come back *early*, you mean?"

Etta pressed hard against the urge to cry. She could not see how things could become any worse. She'd let her frustrations boil over to the very man she'd vowed to crush once she'd become marshal. He now held her fate in his hands, and her father wanted nothing more than to be rid of her.

She stopped outside a door near the gallery entrance and turned to face Nickolas. "It's over. There's no way he'll approve of me in a mere thirty days." It wasn't as if Etta could find a way around it or sully his name. Despite that the man had clearly never even tucked a collar out of place, she needed him in good standing as chancellor in order to bring back her vote. A shaky sigh escaped her. "I'm a fool. Look at me, about to sit for a portrait in the uniform of an office I can never gain. I might as well have them paint over the coat and sword with a leather apron and the tools of an armorer's apprentice." She barely held back a sob. "Or a mobcap and broom."

Nickolas grabbed her by the shoulders and straightened her to face him. "Stop this right now. You're going to march through that door as if you've already won the post. You're going to get painted in that awful jacket that's all the wrong color for you, and you're going to give them the terrifying marshal face I know you practice in your looking glass every night before bed."

She stared at him.

He let go, straightening his own shoulders. "And when you come out, I will be right here, waiting for you. We will commence stealing back what you've earned." She opened her mouth, but he shushed her, pointing a finger in what could only be assumed was a wildly off-precision imitation of a military command. "Not another word. Go."

She did, but only because she was too exhausted to argue.

CHAPTER 5

The entrance hall was dim with only a few candles burning fitfully near the far wall, their light flickering strangely off a row of mirrors. Etta stood quietly for a moment, listening for sounds to indicate the painter was in a connecting room. She heard nothing but the flicker of the candles and the sound of her own breathing. The space was decorated with rich, warm colors, without a single window in view. She walked forward through the narrow room and past her many reflections as they jumped from mirror to mirror alongside her.

Unease niggled at her, and she began to doubt that she'd heard the directions from her father's assistant correctly. If she were late again, for another official appointment... But the thought fell away as the scent of powders and artist's oils met her at the doorway to the next room. She paused inside the entrance, taking in the large, open space cut by shadow and light. The room was littered with props and setups. High windows let in the morning sun, bright and clear over everything it touched. Centered in one square of brilliance was a carved wooden stool, and on the floor around it, various pillows in shades of sapphire, plum, and red. A tasseled scarf was tangled around the legs of the stool, as yellow as one of Lady Narine's birds.

In another square of light stood a valet rack with a dignified officer's coat resting over its arms. Etta walked closer, her eyes tracing the lines of the garment as her footfalls echoed off the far walls. She caught the scent of orange oil and something a bit like musk, but when she glanced through the space, she was still alone. "Lord Barrett?"

No one answered her call, despite the presence of an easel beside a table scattered with what appeared to be freshly prepared paints. She took a final look through the room before her attention was recalled to the coat. The material was dark with red trim and fine gold stitching at the collar and hem. The thing looked as if it might hang off her, as if perhaps it had been a spare sewn for the tall and stoutly built man who currently held the post. A prop for the artist only, and yet, her fingertips trailed reverently over the material. Etta pressed a thumb against a gold button embossed with the office's emblem. *Marshal.* Her dream was so close, she could taste it. But her own actions had driven it from her grasp.

She'd been afraid of her father, afraid he would not let her return. She never should have attempted to outwit the man. She should have faced him in the manner of an officer, one of his own.

She'd wanted to contend with him on her terms. As if such a thing would ever have been possible.

She carefully lifted the coat from its rack, doubling the bulk of it over one arm to straighten a bit of gold stitching.

"Lady Ostwind," came a voice from behind her.

She startled and spun, expecting the portrait artist but instead finding a young man with sandy hair and a freckled nose. At her replied, "Yes," he held forward a letter.

"From Lord Alexander."

Once the message was in her hand, the young man gave a sharp nod and left without another word. Etta shifted the coat to unfold the parchment. A precise script met the heavy dread in her gut, spelling out in detail the task that had been set by the office of the chancery.

Etta stared at the text. The task was a monumental undertaking, impossible for anyone to compete on their own. And yet, the entire kingdom had already attempted it. Every kingsman under her father's command, officer in the current marshal's force, and council member who had a hand in law and order had taken as their responsibility the duty of investigating the noted crime. All had failed.

Etta had been gone from the kingdom for years. She was not yet marshal and had not a single soul under her authority. She'd no chance at all. Gideon knew that and had intentionally given her a task that could not be completed.

The ridges of the chancery's seal caved beneath the pressure of her grip.

Etta stepped backward, leaning heavily upon the stool. Gideon's terms were impossible. She was going to fail and be ruined, and then her father was going to ship her off somewhere far worse than school.

"Antonetta."

The voice was unsettlingly quiet and held a purr, and Etta's gaze snapped up to find its source. A slender man with dark, untidy hair stood in the shadows.

"Lord Barrett?"

His lips tilted up as his head tilted downward in an angle that implied she'd guessed correctly.

She stood.

"No," he replied in a tone just as smooth as his approach, "stay."

She glanced at the high windows, which threw their

brightest light solely over her and the rack that had held the coat, then back at the man. He'd moved to stand by the easel, half hidden by its bulk, his hollow eyes on her. Sitting felt suddenly unnatural. She straightened, shoving Gideon's letter into a pocket of her gown then squaring her shoulders.

"Yes," he said, "just there."

She slid on the oversized jacket, raised her chin, and composed her face in the most esteemed expression she could manage. Her eyes found a spot on the far wall and focused on a bit of cut marble trim that evoked none of the horrible emotions she'd shoved away with the chancellor's letter. There she would sit, Antonetta Ostwind, daughter of the great General Ostwind, as unflinching as her mother, as deserving of the office of marshal as everyone knew she was.

She would make Gideon Alexander eat the parchment his words were printed on.

The artist made another sound like a purr, apparently approving of whatever the posture conveyed from his view. He picked up a brush from the table and began his work without another single word for either Etta or her pose.

ETTA SAT SO until the shadows had slid near her slippered feet, until the sun had angled well past noon. She had not asked once for a break, had not shifted more than a breath as the artist worked. She would sit so for days if that was what it took.

"There." Lord Barrett put down his brush, leaning back to survey the canvas.

Etta blinked, uncertain what precisely *there* meant. "Is that all for today?"

"Come," he beckoned. "It's finished. Tell me what you think of the piece."

Etta stood slowly, surreptitiously stretching limbs that had gone numb. Surely, the portrait could not have been entirely complete, not so quickly, unless he'd used a model for her body, someone sitting for the bulk of the work so that he'd only had to finalize the face. She wasn't certain if artists even did such a thing. She wished she'd paid closer attention, that she'd asked or looked at the canvas before the process had started. But the coat had already been in the room, and she supposed that the man had painted enough official portraits and knew what he needed from her.

She crossed the distance to Lord Barrett, her eyes slow to adjust to the change in light. He gestured toward the canvas, the tilt to his lips widening into something Etta did not quite like. "Your honesty," he told her. "This piece may be the most consequential of your life."

She flinched, snapping her gaze away from him. She'd been so distracted by her anger at Nickolas, what had happened standing before the council, and Gideon's horrendous terms that she hadn't noticed the way the man's teeth did not seem to sit quite properly inside his mouth. It was as if they meant to escape and... well, *bite* her.

Her body shifted as if it intended to move back from him without her command, but her eyes caught sight of the portrait, and she stopped cold.

Etta felt the breath of the man beside her catch. "Stunning, is it not?"

She stared at the portrait, a canvas that rose taller than her. The colors were subdued, a light gray mist covering a backdrop of castle walls and ancient tapestries. The torso and head of a woman centered the image, the coat of marshal fitted well to her straight shoulders and lean form, her hands positioned delicately before her chest. Etta's own eyes stared back at her, her own face bright and hopeful in the center of the frame. It was all that made sense in the portrait, as the rest was... was...

It was absurd. Someone was playing a jape with her, surely. It was why the painting had been completed so quickly. There was no logical reason, no rational excuse for what she was seeing otherwise. Official portraits were so far removed from what was before her that her eyes could not quite decide where to land, what to look at. It was as if a circus had exploded onto the canvas, a troupe of entertainers costuming the figure to gain the most preposterous response possible. A fox peeked out from behind a column in the background, and a shiny red apple rested in the hand of Etta's likeness. Whimsical birds nestled in the cape at her shoulder, and *by the wall*, a black ribbon threaded through her lips, its ends tied into a precise bow.

Lord Barrett sidled closer. "Well," he prompted. "What do you think, Lady Ostwind?"

"There's a goose wrapped about my shoulders and a ship in my hair!"

"Yes," he answered, quiet delight unconcealed in his tone.

"No!" Etta shouted. "This is—it's untenable! Asinine! You've made me look a complete fool!"

The words slipped out before Etta had a moment to realize that they could have been more diplomatic. She couldn't—she just couldn't fathom what had gone wrong. She had to fix it. She had to convince the painter to make it right, to make her look reasonable before anyone saw and she was laughed out of her last chance at the post she so desperately needed.

She glanced at the painter to gauge his response.

He was watching her. After a moment, he asked, "You do not like it?"

Etta swallowed. "I—apologies, my lord, but I feel that the

painting..." She pressed her lips together. "Is it possible to remove the more... playful elements of the work to allow the portrait to better fit with the others? You've seen the other portraits, have you not?" He would surely have painted every single one installed in recent years.

"I have." His expression was hiding some emotion that Etta could not make out while the shadows obscured his face. "They do seem very dull in comparison."

"Yes," Etta told him enthusiastically. "Dull would be perfect. Can you make this more... dull?"

His eyes narrowed on her. "How important is this to you, Lady Ostwind?"

"It is of grave importance. My lord, I would never ask the additional work of you if I did not consider this a matter of utmost urgency. This painting is... well, it's my life."

A rumbling, gratified sound came out of him, somewhere between a laugh and a cry of rejoice. "Indeed," he said. "Do I have your accord, then? It's a bargain?"

"A—" Etta felt her brow draw together in confusion, but at his expectant and encouraging gaze, she nodded vaguely. "Yes, please, my lord. As soon as possible."

Lord Barrett clapped his hands once, the sudden movement and sharp bark of it in the silence startling her a step backward. He did not seem to mind. He hummed delightedly as he turned to the table and unlatched a wooden box inlaid with pearl.

"Here we are," he whispered, attentively drawing a brush from inside. He turned to Etta. "All will be done as agreed. The portrait will appear just as dull as every other that lines the council corridor, and all who look upon it with their dull eyes will see only General Ostwind's daughter, for as you say, this painting for your life."

Etta's mouth came open to reply, but the man stepped

closer, the light catching on his face in a way it had not done before.

"Just one thing more," he murmured as if deep in thought. He raised a hand, and the brush he'd taken from the case brushed her cheek like a feather, the movement fleeting and too quick to escape.

Etta stumbled away from him and tripped over a stack of pillows on the floor. Her face was hot, seared from the touch, and her heart raced. Outside, the screech of a hundred birds rose, their wings and feet battering against the windowpanes as they took frantic flight. Etta caught her fall, steading herself to stare at the hollow eyes of the man before her.

A familiar unease slid through her, followed by a cold, dark surety. He had touched her. And when he had, something had been taken. She couldn't say what, precisely, but she could feel the absence of it. It was thievery, to be sure, and nothing natural.

Etta's body had ordered her to flee before the realization of what was happening had time to settle. Instinct, memory, and the sense her sight gave her that no one else seemed to be willing to accept, those things knew. They understood her mistake.

"Fae," she hissed.

The painter gave her a look that said she was an utter nit.

"What did you do to me?"

He dropped the brush into its case and snapped the lid closed. Then he fastened the clasp, tucked the case under his arm, and gave her a careless glance. "I have taken what is no longer yours."

Fear hit her first, followed swiftly by anger, but it was the fear that drove her to attack. The fae could not be left to escape. Once they crossed the border to their home, one would never be able to reach them again, to steal back what they had taken.

Like when they had taken her mother.

Etta rushed at the man, but his hand went up, and she slammed into a wall of magic as hard as any stone. The impact bloodied her nose. She drew back, her pulse racing in her ears, her fury palpable despite the threat of a powerful fae before her. She wanted to end him.

"What have you taken from me? Give it back, or fates save me, I will destroy you."

His mouth turned into something crueler, something far less human, and she could see that his glamour had been fooling her all along. Her sight had failed for just a few brief glimpses, but those short moments were all it took. She tried frantically to recall what she had said, what words had passed between them.

"A bargain," he answered. "You have traded your life, Lady Ostwind. If you want to see it returned, call his name."

"Who? Whose name?" She needed to know who had done this to her. She could hear the terror in her own voice.

Beneath the beating of her heart, she could hear the answer the painter had not bothered to speak before he turned to go. *Him. It's him.* Not the painter at all, but the fae behind everything, the one they all bowed to, the shadow she had seen as a girl, the one who had taken her mother.

The prince of Rivenwilde.

CHAPTER 6

Etta could see all of him, the artist who was most certainly not Lord Barrett. The creature who'd turned his back on her to walk from the room had let the glamour fall away, his long fingers and smooth gait all that remained of the lord she'd seen before. Something dark like the color of old blood stained the tails of his coat. He was leaving, and she could not let him. Her life, he had said, was in the hands of the fae. The figure shifted into the familiar shape of a shadow, just as it slipped through the door.

He could not be allowed to escape.

Etta made to chase him, but her foot slipped in something slick and dark in the shadows. Among the pillows at her feet, was a form she had not seen. The shape of it could only be that of a man. *Lord Barrett*. Bile rose in Etta's throat, then she picked up a discarded sword near the body and ran.

The entrance hall was no longer dim, as every candle burned hot. The flames blazed, bright and steady, illuminating the mirrors lining the wall in a way that felt endless, as if she were falling. She stumbled once more, off balance, the coat she'd worn hanging from a shoulder. Chest heaving, Etta moved helplessly toward the looking glass, her task forgotten. It might have been a well, its water deep below the rim of stones, calling to her, begging her to fall within.

Magic, some part of her whispered. But the sensation was not caused by the looking glass at all. The magic was closer, hot like the flame of the hundred candles burning around her, alive and stinging on her skin.

She stared into the reflection of a girl in the same dress, the same shoes she'd donned that morning, the same hair. Her hand rose to touch a cheek smeared with paint. Etta's fingers were soft, familiar, so very like what they had always been. She pressed them to the flesh of her cheek, and the glass before her snapped, a long crack splitting the surface in two.

The face—not her own, too round, too soft, too much like a vague and nameless facade, an illusion of glamour like so many the fae wore—stared back at her. A sound somewhere between a sob and a wail crawled from Etta's chest. Her knees gave, but her feet pushed her forward. The next mirror offered another try, and she rushed toward it, saw the girl who was not her, and stared in disbelief. Again, she brushed the flesh of the face with the lightest skim of her fingers. Again, the looking glass shattered.

Etta swore, a vile and ugly string of words that said just what she thought of the fae, that called them out by name. At her shout, every mirror in the room split. Noise crashed through the space as Etta cowered in the center of it, her hands over her ears and her head down to protect a face that was not her own. When the room finally fell quiet, she glanced up. A thousand jagged reflections stared back at her from the floor.

"By the wall," she whispered as Nickolas burst into the room.

He staggered to a stop in the doorway, taking in the shattered glass and Etta's hunkered form before his gaze landed on hers. There was no sign of recognition in him, not a single whit.

She pushed to her feet. "Nickolas!" Whatever she might have asked of him, whatever she might have said, was swallowed by the way he looked at her like a stranger who had no right to know his name.

Her life, the fae had said.

In the endless reflections watching her, she saw a stranger. Realization fell heavily upon her. All the years in which she had seen the cruel tricks of the fae made understanding the depth of their power impossible to ignore.

She hadn't merely been touched by fae magic—it was not some passing jest. Etta had been cursed. Everything that had been hers was, in that brush of fae power, carried off with the monster who'd walked from the room.

Nickolas pushed past her. "Where is Lady Ostwind?" His demand unanswered, he yelled, "Etta!" He rushed into the main room without a backward glance.

Here, her heart whispered. *I am here*. But the words died in her throat, swallowed like all the screams she'd meant to loose as a girl.

The vows she'd made had not gone silent, though. Her fingers curled around the hilt of the sword she'd dropped to the floor beside her. Etta rose, steady on her feet. She would take back what they had stolen. This time, the fae would not win.

CHAPTER 7

The sun, too bright and too hot, was angled in an afternoon sky. Etta had tossed off the marshal's coat outside a castle door, running in slippered feet with no more at her aid than a sword and absolute surety that she had only one chance to stop this catastrophe. Shouts rang out behind her, deep inside the castle walls. She was beyond the notice of the royal guard—she'd escaped by routes few knew of. Her eyes were on the forest ahead.

At the edge of the trees, something chittered, followed by a high-pitched cackle that sounded more like a laugh than any sound an animal should have made. She ran faster, leaping over the stone edging that warned of the encroaching forest then splashing through the narrow creek that wound between the stone and brush. She shot into the tree line, and sweet-briar snagged her hair and dress. Flipping the sword downward, she shoved herself farther past the edge of the woods, snapping limbs and crunching vines and making no secret of her pursuit.

In the distance, a shadow shifted.

"Stop, fae!" The shout echoed through the forest, sending

birds to flight and scattering small prey. She ran beneath the cacophony, the chaos of limbs and brambles thinning as she went deeper into the woods. She had her feet again, and she did not waste the advantage, running as fast as she was able toward a creature who had no need of haste.

The fae strode through the forest without looking back at her. What little light filtered through the canopy dappled his form and revealed glints of color with every new step.

"Halt!" she shouted, furious that the word held no true weight of command.

The shadow did not stop but moved deeper into the woods, forcing Etta to follow. She was gaining on him, but he turned too swiftly, and she nearly lost him between the trees. She struggled past a thicket of spiny shrubs then turned to free whatever had snagged on her skirts. It was not a branch, as she expected. A low, slinky, furred *thing* smiled up at her, its teeth a row of spikes like shards of glass. She shrieked, raised her sword to strike, and nearly came off balance as it sprung at her. Its claws were dug well into her skirts, and the horrid thing was too close to get a good swing in. Faster than should have been possible, it scampered up her body, drawing the length of her caught skirt on its way then tumbling them both backward over a log.

Etta landed on her back with a grunt, swinging her sword arm up just as the creature launched itself free and took a hunk of her skirt with it right over her head. She smacked the fabric down from her face, rolled onto her knees, and jumped to her feet. She went after the thing, bruising a shoulder on a tree before breaking through to a dark clearing.

She froze, chase abandoned, to stare up at a massive struc-ture that seemed to stretch the length of the forest. Her mouth gaped in awe, and her heart did a strange little dance in her chest. Magic thrummed through the ground beneath her, as if she stood on the bank of a river and could feel its current, as if the mud beneath her feet might fall in at any moment to be swept along with the flow.

Rising from blue mossy earth before her was a wall as ancient as Westrende. Like so much tied to the fae, it appeared as lovely and harmless as the common pale stone it mimicked. But Etta could see the truth. Beneath the flowering vines that appeared to roll softly over its surface waited bloody thorns as sharp as blade. Where one might have seen the face of the stone as smooth, Etta could make out delicate curves and twists of iron, the metal ties that bound the fae.

The wall sat upon the Rive, a boundary between the fae wilds and Westrende. Those ancient knots of metal were all that kept the fae out—all that was *supposed* to keep them from coming through and all that kept an unsuspecting human from stumbling into the fae realm.

Some small thing bounded from a tree behind her, and Etta's gaze swung down the wall. Not thirty paces from her stood the shadow who had posed as her artist, the man who had taken her face.

He was as still as the stone, glancing at her only briefly before moving to step toward the wall.

Etta launched herself at him, her grip firm about her raised sword.

His attention came back to her, revealing in its true form the same wicked smile he'd given her in the castle. "Call his name," the fae reminded her, "and discover what trade it might take to see your precious life returned."

The echo of his laughter was all she heard as her sword struck where he had been, the wall as solid as if he'd not just walked through.

"No!" she screamed, pummeling the stone with sword and fist. She'd had one chance, one single hope of regaining her life.

It was gone. Once the fae she'd just lost delivered the box

that held her curse to the prince of Rivenwilde, Etta was doomed. She did not need to hear his taunting laugh to understand that. There would be no trade at all that she could make with fae royalty, and calling the prince would only bring him to retrieve the box that much sooner. Etta knew better than to believe they would give her a chance. She swore, the wall flickering beneath hands she realized had gone bloody.

She snatched her fists back, watching as the magic seemed to sap her blood. It crackled icily, a flower blooming at the site of one drop, its petals unfurling in the short moment Etta held her breath. Stepping back, she watched as more vines expanded like metal skeletons. But through the glamour, they appeared as elaborate carved stone. Pale fingers rose from the smooth surface, a sculpture unsettlingly like Etta's own hand. It wrapped about the newly formed blossom, grasping in a manner so desperate it made her heart ache.

She took another step back, her stomach turning. Fates protect her, she was standing unguarded before the Rive. Her gaze flicked down the facade, the horror of what each carving meant becoming painfully clear. Just beyond the flowering vines, a half-formed figure of smooth stone had risen, the shape of a man who appeared caught stepping through, frozen in time and only partially emerged, his features as finely formed as any sculpture in the castle. His hands were wrapped around the reins of a horse, its stone head thrown back and nostrils flared. Tendrils of the animal's mane curled outward, catching in the vines and thorns that fell over the top of the wall.

Etta blinked away the images and swung back toward the forest with her heart pounding. Lesser fae watched her, perched in trees and tucked beneath piles of earth. None wore glamour in the safety of the woods. Unafraid, eager, they waited for her next move.

A hasty swallow stuck in her throat. She gripped the

sword tighter. A long vine reached out from the wall and brushed her shoulder. She jerked away from it, tearing another piece of fabric. She ran, full force, into the trees.

ETTA'S LEGS did not want to carry her farther, but she had little choice but to keep on. It had not been a long walk from the castle to the wall, but she wasn't foolish enough to misunderstand how she'd found it so quickly.

She had no shadows to follow anymore. She could not trust whatever lesser fae interrupted her journey to see her out of the forest—they would have led her deeper, forcing her to become more entangled in the mess and the magic of the greenwood. She couldn't stop to rest. She had to get out, return to the castle before nightfall, make a plan, and find some way to cross through the wall. She had to get her life back.

"There you are."

The voice jolted Etta so profoundly that she was swinging her sword before she realized she knew whose voice it was. Nickolas ducked, and her blow missed him by a hair. He grabbed hold of her, but it was not the embrace of a friend.

Nickolas was holding her captive. He stared down at her, his hand twisted in the material at the shoulder of her gown. Etta was so taken aback by his manner that she let him remove the sword from her aching hand.

"Where is she?" His tone was remarkably cold.

Etta opened her mouth to reply but could not find a single word. She could barely fathom what she had just been through.

"Lady Ostwind," Nickolas demanded. "Where is she?"

Etta's mouth snapped closed. She recalled Nickolas having

found her among the shattered glass outside the portrait room. When he'd gone inside to search, Etta had not been there. "She's—Nickolas, it's me. I'm her."

Something passed over his expression as he leaned closer. "I don't know how you know my name, but if you have hurt her—"

"Don't be ridiculous. I'm telling you, it's me. Etta." She was yanked nearer and smacked at his hand—ineffectually, it turned out, because she was quite tired and Nickolas was quite strong. "Let go of me."

He turned, tugging her toward what she abruptly realized was the edge of the forest. She sagged in relief, and he turned back again, evidently deciding she meant to resist his capture. He drew a strap from his pocket then yanked her nearer to snatch her wrist.

She gasped, twisted, and spun free of him, only to fall face first to the forest floor when her torn skirt was ripped further by his grip. He leapt on top of her, pressing her into the earth. She growled, wrapped a leg about his ankle, and rolled them both. Off balance, Nickolas was a much easier opponent to manage, but he still outsized her by half. His cursed lanky arms trapped her in a solid hold before she could escape.

"I'm too exhausted for this!"

He stared down at her.

"Get off me, you lout." Limbs going limp, Etta sighed. "Fine. I'll explain it from here."

"Do," he said, "and quickly."

The afternoon sun was nowhere in sight. If Etta had to guess, they had less than an hour before sunset, and they were still on the wrong side of the tree line.

"It was a setup. The portrait artist was not Lord Barrett at all. I was a fool. I should have noticed. But I was so distracted, and so"—she shook her head—"he put me in the painting somehow. Touched me with a brush, and I knew it was magic and what—what did he say? *The painting for your life.* Then my face was gone. I felt it. I just didn't know what had happened until I saw the mirrors. I chased after him, but I wasn't fast enough. Now, he's gone, and I'm gone, and I just need to go home so I can get into my father's study, search his books, and find a way over that blasted wall."

Nickolas only blinked. After a moment, he stood and shook his pant leg straight before tugging Etta to her feet. "All right," he said. "Time to go."

Go. He meant to take her—as what, she wasn't sure. A prisoner, perhaps, if he truly thought she'd done something to the missing Etta.

"Nickolas, why am I in restraints?" she demanded.

His expression said he was entirely done with their conversation, and maybe that he wished she would stop calling him by his given name. "My lady, it appears you were the last known witness at the scene of a heinous crime. It is my duty, as a citizen of the great kingdom of Westrende, to hand you over to the marshal."

A boulder dropped in Etta's stomach. Her knees felt as if they might not hold her weight. "Lord Barrett," she whispered.

"Indeed. Now, you can come along willingly, or I can drag you to the edge of this forest and whistle for a guard to haul you back, strapped like luggage to the rump of his horse. I recommend the former."

"No. It's not what you think. Please, Nickolas, just listen to me. Just"—she cursed. "I did not murder Lord Barrett."

His blue eyes, as earnest as she'd ever seen, met hers. "The truth is, whoever you are, I care not at all about the lord in that hall." His voice lowered. "I care about finding Lady Ostwind."

"Nickolas."

Her word was barely above a whisper, her heart warming

until Nickolas tugged his lapel straight and added, "She needs to clear my good name."

Something horrid rose in Etta, that same boiling, awful heat that she felt toward the fae. Whatever nasty word that slipped free from her mouth, Nickolas only had time to look momentarily appalled before she took him to the ground. "You dirty, self-serving, absolute boor of a man! I swear to the wall, I will gut you and string your insides out for the birds, you no good—"

Beneath her, Nickolas's grappling suddenly stilled. Etta froze, too, afraid for a moment that they'd waited too long and the forest had come alive. But it was only her words— that Etta had threatened him with the birds.

"Yes," she whispered. "Nickolas, it's me." She shuffled off him, trying fervently to explain it all again. It took longer this time, though her mind was a tangle and Etta herself could barely believe it was real.

"The painting," he repeated. The disbelief was so plain in his voice that she might have thrown up her hands in defeat. But she needed him. To add insult to injury, her hands were bound.

She needed someone, just one lousy soul to believe her. Nickolas was that lousy soul.

"Exactly. The painting. It was hideous. I said so." She wiped a lock of hair back from her face with an arm. Her fingers were trembling, her wrists burning from the cord. "And he turned to me and..." And she had seen. She had known. By the wall, she should have run when she'd had the chance. "It was him." Her voice had gone tremulous. There was nothing else she could say. If Nickolas didn't believe her, if someone didn't come to her aid...

"You're saying he was fae?"

Etta's head shot up. "Yes. Oh, saints, Nickolas, I'm so glad you believe me. I can't—"

He held up a hand to stop her. "My lady, I feel that we are both overwrought. Perhaps you believe entirely what you are telling me, but the truth is, it's impossible to credit. Magic does not exist in Westrende. Fae don't walk the castle halls, pretending to be lords. You may have been involved with Lady Ostwind's disappearance, but you most certainly are not her."

"I can prove it."

He crossed his arms. "I don't have time for this nonse—"

"You have a scar on your right thigh."

Nickolas gave her a patronizing look. "That's not exactly a state secret, is it?"

Etta leaned closer, voice dropping to something mean. "It's long and narrow. A slice that skinned you of your trousers while you shimmied not from Lady Asha's balcony in a hasty escape, as you like to boast, but from your own mother's garden wall because you thought she was after you with a switch."

His mouth went flat.

"There's another on your hip. No one sees it, not these days, but when you were two and ten, you jumped from the roof of the old smokehouse, trying to catch a pig. You caught him. He pummeled you and took a bite out of your haunch. You couldn't wear your sword for a week. Made up a tale about it when the other boys saw you swimming bare-cheeked in the watering hole beyond the west gate."

He went pale.

Etta took a step forward. "And your left ear." She raised a brow. "It's smaller than the right."

Nickolas drew a breath as if he'd been slapped.

"That's right," she told him. "I can do this all day."

"You cannot be seri—"

"Try me," Etta said.

The look on his face was utterly unstable. Wearing her

own skin, Etta had never pushed Nickolas so far—it did little good, as he knew her weaknesses too. But this girl, this crazed, disheveled mess of a thing, she was something that Nickolas didn't understand.

"You owe me." Etta's voice was as hard as steel. "You owe me, and you agreed to help me." Her finger found his chest, poking him right over the gilded trim. "You didn't tell me the man I stumbled into in the corridor upon our return was Gideon Alexander, when you knew full well that I would be facing him at the council meeting that would decide my fate. You let me fail, Nickolas. And for that, I call in my due."

He shifted nearly imperceptibly, something like guilt rising in the softness of his expression, threatening to overtake the disbelief.

She moved in for the kill. "You will help me, or I will report to the council the thing you did on Harvest Day."

His jaw went slack, his sharp eyes snapping to scan the clearing as if someone might have overheard.

Etta leaned back, hands on her hips as if she'd already won —hands that she'd freed from his tether without his notice and right beneath his nose. He looked at her again, clearly noting the set of her shoulders and the tap of her finger on her side. *You*, she made certain the posture said, *have been beaten*. It was the manner in which Lady Ostwind had often stood.

"You," he breathed.

"Yes," Etta answered. "Me."

CHAPTER 8

"You can't just walk back into that wing of the castle." Nickolas's words held a hint of lingering disbelief.

She didn't have time to finish convincing him of everything she understood about fae and magic. "What else am I supposed to do? I need to sort this out, Nickolas. I have to get that box, end that fae, and return with my own face in time to..." She sighed. "In time to fail at completing the chancellor's task."

"One failure at a time."

She gave him a look. He winced, apparently put off by her mannerisms on someone else's face.

"The chancellor wants me to discover what's behind the string of misfortunes and illnesses that have befallen our prospects for king," she said.

Nickolas gaped at her.

"I know. It's inconceivable." She picked a thorny twig from the material of her skirt. "The only thing I can do is gather the existing evidence, make a thorough report of every prior inquiry's failures, and hope that it's enough. Hope that he recognizes the work I put in and sees that I'm serious, capable, and not a fool cavorting with a known rake in the staff corridors."

Nickolas placed a hand on his chest, opened his mouth as if he might defend his reputation, then apparently thought better of it. "Will that be enough?" he asked instead.

"I don't know." She ran a hand over her face. "It's all I have."

He shook his head. "I think I can help but... I'm not certain what—by the wall, I cannot believe I'm considering any part of this. I must have lost my mind."

"You haven't. It's me beneath this mask. That's my disappointment in your character you're seeing, just like always."

"Shrew."

"Lout."

His mouth twisted thoughtfully. "The groom's entrance. There's a corridor that lets out near the south end of the chapel."

"Perfect."

It was not perfect, but it had done. They'd managed to deliver Etta to her rooms without drawing notice from a single kingdom official. Then Nickolas had run like the coward he was, which was fine. She had much to do.

The door snicked quietly closed behind her, and Etta let her gaze sweep the room. Castle staff had already been in, lighting candles and leaving a dish of food on a table in the sitting room, despite that she'd gone missing. She grabbed a roll before even washing her hands then paced farther into the room. Beyond the doorway, evening light spilled in through the window of her bedroom, illuminating the floor in the spot where she had watched the fae prince seize hold of her mother so many years before.

Do not speak of them. Speak of them, and they will come again.

The bread turned to ash in her mouth. She dropped what

was left of the roll onto the mantel and knelt before her trunk. She'd meant to gather a clean gown, but a glint of metal caught her eye. She reached into the pocket that held her jewelry, taking hold of the chain that had worked free during their travels. It was her mother's locket. Inside were two tiny paintings, one of a young Etta and one of her father.

She stood and crossed to the vanity table, where she settled atop the fine cushioned stool, still in a torn, filthy gown. She turned the looking glass toward the face she wore. A stranger's features stared miserably back. It was fairly torturous to look upon oneself as someone else, and Etta felt downright wretched, overall. But she was back in her rooms, among old memories, and she would use what she'd learned to dig her way out. She was ready. *Always ready.*

The glamour flickered over her skin. Its illusion would fool any single human who looked at her—any human, Etta supposed, who was not able to see through the magic like she could.

Etta wasn't certain when she'd realized others could not see the truth, some whispered word, probably, or some warning from her father. Her flesh was still her own, which was a comfort, but only she would be aware of that. The magic couldn't change her actual form and couldn't make her someone else, but it had changed how others would see her. The fae had taken as much of her identity as they could.

Glamour was not their only tool. Since she was a child, Etta had watched fae walk through the halls of the castle, unmasked, their magic diverting the attention of any who passed. But to interact, they needed more, something that convinced the public that they'd seen only a common man, nothing out of the ordinary. The illusions were always as plain as a human might come, purposefully forgettable.

Etta recalled her mother saying long ago that too great a beauty came with unpleasant rewards, the sort of attention that got in the way. "You, my darling girl, are the precise amount of loveliness that means many will look upon you with admiration, but not so much that the beauty inside of you will not also be allowed to shine. Whatever it is that you set your heart on, it will be yours. I'm confident of it." She had smiled, brushing a thumb softly over Etta's cheek. In the looking glass, she saw her own hand rise and brush a cheek that wanted others to see nothing of that girl at all.

The mirror shattered. Glass clinked against the table in shards, a scattered mess so much like the one in the hall outside the portrait studio.

She cursed the fae. She cursed their cursed curse.

Behind her, the door to the room swung open. Etta turned to find a maid standing in the doorway, taking in the scene with apparent shock. "All is well," Etta began, forgetting for a moment that she did not have her own face.

She was not allowed to forget for long. The maid shouted, picked up a candle holder, and rushed at Etta.

"I couldn't just walk back into that wing of the castle."

Nickolas crossed his arms, giving Etta a flat look.

She shrugged. "A maid tried to have me arrested for breaking into to the lady Ostwind's rooms. I barely escaped. She was absolutely vicious. 'How dare I sneak into the room of the venerated general's daughter and steal her bread rolls.' Nearly ended up in chains. Thank the fates for the hours of running they put me through during training. Can you imagine the incoming marshal being put into irons?"

Nickolas blinked.

She moved past him to flop onto a chaise in his absurdly extravagant sitting room. "I need a place to stay."

"No." He shook his head, his finger, and apparently the thoughts right out of his mind, because he only stood there, staring at her as she sprawled over his furniture.

"You owe me," she said.

He pursed his lips.

"Oh, I see. As Lady Ostwind, I'm perfectly marriageable and all you ever wanted, but suddenly, I have nothing, and you won't risk being caught with me in your rooms."

"You're a fugitive," he reminded her.

She kicked her earth-smeared feet up onto his table. "You're the only witness that this face was even there. For all we know, *you* killed Lord Barrett."

His eyes narrowed. "No. Nay. Certainly not. This isn't happening. I will find a place for you to stay, but that place is *not* here."

Etta drew her feet down, sitting up to look at him. "So I've convinced you fully, then? You believe at the very least that this is me?" He did not quite believe the fae were in Westrende, but she chose to ignore that.

He squeezed his eyes shut for a long moment. "Yes. You can stop your bullying and acting the tormentor. I yield."

A relieved breath slid from her. "Thank all that is agreeable. How do you tolerate being so indecorous all the time? It makes my neck twitch."

Nickolas's head dropped back to stare at the ceiling. "It's a gift."

She was quiet for a moment, letting him adjust to their new reality. Eventually, he came back to center, dropping his arms to his sides in defeat. He leaned against the arm of a puffy embroidered chair. "What is the plan?"

Her expression might have been sober, but Etta felt the first bubbles of hope rising in her chest. "I need access to my father's study. One book in particular. Clearly, that won't happen with me looking like..." She gestured vaguely to her face. "His rooms are far more protected even than the king's suite."

"That's because there's no king in them."

"And beside the point. I need that book to find a way through the wall."

Nickolas stood. "No! Why—what is wrong with you? Have you entirely lost your senses? You plan to go through the wall?"

"They *stole my face*, Nickolas. My life. If don't get it back —" A sound of pure misery crawled out of her chest. "If I don't get it back and soon, I'll not only never be Antonetta Ostwind. I'll never be marshal."

"It's disturbing the order of importance you've put on those things. You realize that, do you not?"

She frowned. "I do. It doesn't change anything."

He paced back to the chair then sat to perch on its edge, his thinking face firmly in place. "So you need access to well-protected documents, and you also need to complete the chancellor's task."

"Yes. And quickly."

"Without the use of your own face."

She pressed her fingers hard against her temple. It did not make the headache go away.

Nickolas nodded. "Feasible. You'll need fresh clothes. But —and I can't believe I'm saying this at the state of you—don't clean up."

CHAPTER 9

"**Y**ou'll see." Nickolas had told her of his plan that she go to the chancery's office as bedraggled as she'd come into his rooms. He'd allowed her to sleep in his suite but had tucked her into a closet on a blanket, the door nearly closed. It wasn't much more absurd than anything else that had happened since the dawn before, but as Etta stood outside the office of chancery with a forged letter of reference from Nickolas's distant cousin, she had serious doubts that she would succeed at anything outside of being arrested.

A waif of a girl with an arm full of scrolls rushed past, nearly knocking into Etta as if she'd not noticed her at all. A few steps beyond, though, and the girl froze, her shoulders straightening as she turned to face Etta head on. One of the scrolls tumbled from her arms, rolling across the floor before knocking into a door frame.

"May I help you find something?" Her hair was slightly disheveled, her big brown eyes earnest despite that she was clearly in a rush.

Etta managed not to out with her standard introduction

of "Antonetta Ostwind," but only barely. Moving a step forward so that her voice was less likely to echo through the chamber beyond, she began, "I'm here for—" She had to stop, clear her throat, and force a lesser confidence into her tone. "I was told there was a position available as secretary?"

"Secret—oh, well. That's unexpected. The prior secretary has just left us, as a matter of fact. I'm surprised word is already out, frankly. It all happened in a bit of a rush. But yes, she's to be married, so there will be no more flitting around the stacks for her."

"She was removed from the position for becoming engaged?"

The girl's cheeks colored. "Oh, no. Not at all. No one minds if staff is married. I blame her fall from the library ladder."

Etta blinked.

"Broke her leg in several places. The doctor informed her she was not to climb another ladder as long as she was under his care."

"It never healed properly?"

The girl looked at her as if she were slow-witted, and Etta was beginning to feel as if she might be. "She's to be married to the doctor," the girl explained.

"I see," Etta said, though she did not. Her confidence in Nickolas's plan was taking a hard dive into murky water. She wasn't certain she'd get into the chancery at all.

Shifting her burden into one arm and consequently dropping two more scrolls, the girl added, "I'm Jules. Clerk's assistant, notary's assistant..." She waived a hand, as if to encompass all the assisting not theretofore mentioned. "Come along, and I'll get you to the proper desk."

The proper desk, it turned out, was vacant.

"Robert," Jules called. "Where is the clerk?"

A freckled, sandy-haired young man popped his head out

from behind a tall shelf. Etta's stomach flipped in recognition —he was the boy who'd delivered her message from Gideon, right before things had gone so horribly wrong.

He barely glanced at Etta, his eyes skimming over her with no sign of recognition. It was precisely how the fae illusions were meant to work.

"Out for the day," he said of the clerk.

Jules nodded briskly then led Etta through the next room.

The chancery's office remained in an older wing of the castle, likely because no one was interested in relocating the sheer volume of records it held. Every wall supported shelf after shelf of books, and every flat surface was stacked with more. Document carts and scroll baskets scattered a space that smelled somewhat of rusk and leather beneath slightly musty air. It was strangely charming and intimate, despite the grandeur. She'd been sent to fetch books from the stacks as a girl, her history tutor claiming he no longer had the legs to make the trip. It had seemed so much larger then. Now, her task loomed impossibly higher before her.

"My lord," Jules called as they came into a new chamber.

"One moment," a voice replied from somewhere beyond another rack of shelves.

"I've found a lost soul," Jules said toward the voice's general direction. "She's looking to apply for the position of secretary, if you can believe it."

Etta came to a dead stop, unease crawling up her neck.

"Secretary? Jules, you know we no longer need someone for that post." The face that peered around the rack was perplexed, then at the sight of Etta, suddenly became distressed. The chancellor opened his mouth as if to shout a warning, and Etta's stomach pitched.

She was certain he saw through the fae glamour, and she could feel the last chance at the only thing that might win her life back slipping from her grasp. And again, all because of *him*, the stupid fool man with his stupid dark eyes and—she screamed when a giant beast leapt from the darkness, knocking her straight to the ground. It was massive and hairy and wiggling, and by the fates, it had too many arms. Shouts rang through the room as she struggled beneath the monster without sword or weapon, her own limbs ineffectual as its reeking mouth found her face, hot and wet and—

A sound like *oof* slipped out of her when it slammed the full weight of its bottom half right atop her gut. The other end settled firmly on her chest and shoulders, its gaping maw inches from her nose.

"Clara!" one of voices scolded, closer this time, and the great vigorous beast was hauled off Etta's chest.

She gasped for breath, unable to move outside of a generalized shaking.

"Please, Jules, please just take her outside."

Etta caught sight of Jules, stock still with her slender hands covering her mouth. Her eyes were wider than ever, her cheeks gone pale.

The dark-robed figure of Gideon Alexander held the collar of what Etta realized was an enormous dog. He passed possession of the beast to Jules, despite the girl's diminutive frame. The dog hopped once, excitedly trying to lick at Jules's face, then was led from the room as if such was an everyday occurrence.

Etta stared after them, still prone and with no intention of rising.

Gideon moved to stand beside her, and for a terrifying moment, Etta expected a declaration that he recognized her, that the whole ordeal had been some sort of jest. But he only leaned down, taking hold of her arm to help her to her feet. His grip slid down her forearm as they straightened, and he did not immediately let go of her trembling hand.

"Are you well?" he asked, his gaze remaining solely on her eyes.

"No," she answered automatically then swallowed and shook her head. "I mean yes, I'm unharmed."

"Please, allow me to apologize. Clara is only—well, she adores meeting new people. I keep her tucked away in a spare office when we have visitors, but with Jules and the others..." One of his shoulders raised in the slightest shrug. "She's used to them. They're used to her. She meant you no harm. She's a darling, truly."

Clara. The beast that had mauled her had the sort of soft, sweet name that sounded as if it belonged to someone's favorite aunt.

Gideon's other hand came to rest beneath Etta's elbow. His head tilted as he examined her face. "Are you certain you're well?"

Etta realized she was still shaking. She realized he was still holding her hand. She snatched the hand back, running her palms over her borrowed skirt, a garment that Nickolas had said made her look properly indigent. "I'm sorry. I must seem a fool. It's only that I really needed the post."

The post that was no longer available. The man before her, the man who'd just held her hand, had given her a task that would have been impossible even as a general's daughter. It would be unimaginable with a stranger's face and no ties to the kingdom. Nickolas had been right. Taking a post in the chancery's office was her only way out. She needed access to her father's documents, and she needed to be close to Gideon to complete his ludicrous challenge. There were no second chances with council beyond the one they'd given her.

And it seemed she'd just failed.

"My lady." Gideon's voice was soft, and Etta realized she'd been silent for far too long while he contemplated her.

She tugged the sleeve of her gown to cover the scratches

on her arm from the fight with a lesser fae and a half dozen brambles.

The chancellor pretended not to notice. "Did you tell me your name?"

"Etta." Something like a flinch went through him, and she stuttered. "For Margaretta. It was—my grandmother—it was her name." She dipped an awkward quarter-curtsy to hide her flush. "Please, call me Etta."

He didn't seem to mind that she was flustered as her eyes rose again to his. He only watched her calmly, his lips pressed together. Saints protect her, she wanted to hate him. She wanted to want to smash his perfect pensive face.

"Margaretta," he said, "perhaps I can find something for you to do."

CHAPTER 10

Come evening, Etta was settled into the staff lodging for the chancery's office with Jules in the bunk opposite her and young Robert and another man in an adjoining room. She'd been aware, growing up with so many tutors and in proximity to her father, that many who worked inside the castle did not live among the luxury of Etta's personal rooms. But she'd always assumed anyone who worked for the kingdom lived well. She had grossly over-supposed.

"It's perfectly lovely, isn't it?" Jules smiled as she wrapped her arms around a threadbare pillow and leaned back against the dark-paneled wall of their room. Her booted feet were curled beneath her, her posture so at ease that it was clear she felt the statement to be entirely true.

Surrounding them was ancient wood, spare of trim, none of it polished and oiled but worn with age. The room held no fireplace, no window, and would be as black as pitch when Jules put out the single light, never mind that it smelled a bit too much like the dull-gray bird whose cage was perched on the nightstand against Jules's bed.

Etta's throat felt tight. "I've never been more pleased." It was true, but only because of the immense relief flooding her after coming so close to missing a post in the chancery. Her fingers curled into the scratchy blanket covering her bunk. She had not a single possession aside from the locket she had taken from her trunk and Gideon's letter detailing her task. Even her gown was borrowed, a fact she'd been too distracted to follow up on at the time, though she was sure Nickolas had managed a delightful excuse for whomever he'd borrowed it from.

Jules tugged a chunk of bread from her pocket and carefully fed pieces of it to the squawking bird through the bars of its cage. Her fingers no more than slid free of its reach before the thing's frantic flapping started up again.

"There you go," Jules cooed, passing over the last of her supply. "A few more weeks, and you'll be as good as new."

The creature's wing was at an angle that did not appear to support the promise, but Etta held her tongue. "So up at cockcrow to ready the rooms, meals in the back office, and casual dress. Is there anything more I need to know?"

Jules's dark eyes met hers. "Robert and I will ready the rooms. We've no need of your help for that. You can get started a little later, as the chancellor prefers a bit of private time in the mornings."

"What does that have to do with me?"

"You'll not want to disturb him." She waved a hand as if the details were inconsequential. "You'll catch on soon enough. I've confidence in you, my lady. It won't be long before you have free run of the place. I'm sure of it. Get some sleep now. I'll lend you a gown so you might get that one washed. No worries this evening, I'll lay it out for you when morning comes."

Etta glanced down at her dress. The seams pulled in two

spots where she'd hastily tied it on inside Nickolas's closet. Her fingers were twisted in the ribbon at her waist, hands scratched from the fae, and nails dark with earth from her tussle with Nickolas on the forest floor. By the wall, she'd too much to do. She needed to find a way out of the chancery's wing and into her father's office. She hoped Jules was right that she would have a bit of freedom soon. She glanced up to ask another question and found Jules fast asleep, her dress still bound to her slender frame, boots laced tightly where they stuck out from beneath her hem. The bird sat silently, head tucked into its neck, the occasional twitch the only sign it was aware of Etta.

Etta stood, carefully lowered the drape over the cage, then snuffed out the light. In the darkness, she stepped cautiously back to her bunk. Her shin bumped against the edge, as it was impossibly near. She sighed, untied her gown, stripped down to her shift, then crawled into bed to stare up at the darkness. She would not tell Nickolas she preferred his closet. She would not think of how easily she might sneak in and smother the head of chancery in his sleep.

"What do you mean?" Etta hissed. "The secretary doesn't work directly with the chancellor."

Jules grinned at her with that same pleasant smile that could not have been as consistently genuine as it seemed. "Normally, no. But you've no experience as a secretary, now, do you? He can train you. Besides, I think you should give Lord Alexander a chance. You might like him."

"Like him?"

"The work, I mean. Chancellor is certainly a more interesting post than secretary. Experience it while you have the chance. And he's the only one who has time."

Etta's eyes narrowed. The girl had left her a decent gown, as promised, and had come into their room as chipper as a new chick, eager to usher Etta to her station. But every word that came out of her mouth felt as misleading as the last.

"You're saying the head of chancery has more time than—"

"Off you go." Jules shooed Etta through the doorway, leaving her with no more than a little wave and a wish of luck as she hurried in the opposite direction. "Don't fall off any ladders!"

Etta stood silently inside the door to the chancellor's office, staring after Jules. Then quite suddenly, she recalled the giant dog Gideon had said he kept locked inside. She spun, expecting at any moment to be laid out once more, and found the chancellor of Westrende, dressed not in the robes he so often wore but in the official coat of his station. It was fitted to his form with square shoulders, the high collar done all the way up, and the buttons gleaming and polished despite the sparse light. At his side, a slender sword hung. In his hand, he held a piece of parchment.

"My lady."

Etta's gaze jerked back to his face. She wasn't certain whether she was meant to curtsy. She didn't think she would. He was her last chance at freedom, though, so she dipped her head. "Lord Alexander."

"Gideon."

She gave a brief nod, hating the way polite familiarity tasted in her mouth. "Gideon." He stood there a moment more, and she had the sense that he'd forgotten entirely that he'd offered her a post. "Where shall I get started?"

He made the smallest little head shake then took a breath.

"I was on my way to a meeting. But I'll just"—he held up the document—"let me send this with Robert, and I'll be right back. We'll figure something out."

He walked past, a whisper of woodruff hitting Etta before it disappeared among the scent of stale documents. *We'll figure something out?* She prayed he would not change his mind. Of course he hadn't had the time Jules had promised. She couldn't understand why he had even let her stay.

Etta walked farther into the room, taking in a well-loved desk stacked with layers of official-looking correspondence and a neat pile of blank parchment beside wax and seal. She ran a finger over the edge of the quill feather, black as his robes and its vane just as pristine. Her gaze trailed up a wall of books beyond the desk and down another beside it. Records and rules. Every law the kingdom had ever known. He spent his days surrounded by the code she, as marshal, was meant to uphold.

Etta turned slowly, memorizing the space.

When she noticed Gideon's return, she straightened, waiting for him with a posture she realized too late was probably overly militant for her stint as Margaretta. She wasn't sure how to soften herself but made an effort.

Gideon stopped inside the room and looked around, the edge of his lip tucked beneath his teeth. His eyes landed on a stack of crates by the far wall. "There we are." He gestured toward the mess, not hiding the that-should-keep-you-occupied-for-a-day-or-two note to his tone.

He intended to keep her toiling away at busywork, then, not train her as secretary. And there, inside his office. Her carefully laced fingers tightened, but she managed a civil smile. She had to be grateful for any chance to win back her life, even if she would have to do it right under his nose. "Of course. I'll get to work right away."

He nodded, apparently satisfied, and went back to his desk. Etta moved a chair closer to the crates to begin her work. She would sit pleasantly, looking as busy as he wanted, but the moment Gideon left her alone, her true tasks would begin.

CHAPTER 11

They sat in easy silence until Etta's eyes were sore and her fingers covered in dust from the sorting. Gideon had not left his post once. When Jules fetched Etta for a brief meal with the rest of the staff, Gideon took the opportunity to run off for a meeting. He was back before the others had let Etta out of her sight. It was as if they didn't quite trust her, despite that they'd taken her on without a single check of the poorly constructed background she and Nickolas had thrown together or of her character.

The afternoon went similarly, the quiet shuffle of paper the only sound for so long that when Gideon finally spoke, it came almost as a surprise that she wasn't alone. She glanced up at him behind his desk, much more put together than she was with documents strewn across her lap and in newly made piles on the various crates and shelves around her.

"Enough for today," he said. The light coming in through the windows had faded, evening apparently having arrived without her notice. In the candlelight, the gold of Gideon's collar gleamed—still done up to the neck, not a stitch out of place on his person—but there was a little twist to the lock of hair at his temple, which curled down to brush his skin. She drew her gaze from it when his tone became a dismissal. "It looks as if you've made good progress. You can start again in the morning, same time."

She began the next morning, the same task in the same chair. She was certain the chancellor had other duties to perform, that he would not normally spend all day hunched over his desk. But by midafternoon of the third day, Etta felt as if she'd been a problem forced upon him, that her presence had somehow changed the entire chancery staff's schedules.

They'd made room for her. She needed less of it.

"Robert," Gideon called from the corner of the office. He was in the coat again, his shoulders set in the way of a person who had far too much to do and no time in which to do it.

"He's gone out," Jules answered, peeking her head around the doorframe with bundles of rolled parchment in each arm. "Won't be back for hours."

"Tobias, then."

Jules shook her head. "Not feeling well." Her eyes flicked briefly to Etta. "Nothing serious, but I've sent him to his rooms for a bit."

Gideon frowned. "That's twice this month."

"He'll be all right." Jules's voice was firm, but her grip on the rolled parchment, not so much. One fell to the floor and rolled into the distance. "What is it that you need?"

He sighed. "It's only a letter for the exchequer. I'll not trouble you with it."

Etta stood. "I can deliver the letter."

They both glanced at her, Gideon's expression almost offensively uncertain.

"It's no problem. I know precisely where his office is. I can have it delivered before Robert even returns." When he didn't immediately reply, she added, "And it will get me out of your hair for a bit." The smile she gave him was probably not quite as self-deprecating as she intended, but she did try.

His thumb slid over the parchment. Eventually, he held the letter forward. "It's not entirely vital. I'm sure you'll do well enough."

She took the proffered letter, hoping he meant it wasn't important enough to merit someone with a higher level of security delivering the thing and not that he fully expected her to cock it up. She didn't have the luxury of being offended, in any case—she needed out of the chancery wing, and running messages might be her only way.

Gideon gave her one final look before turning back to his work. Etta didn't wait for him to change his mind.

Etta's route to the exchequer's office took her down the corridor outside council chambers and through the long, wide passage that was strung with portraits of Westrende officials. It felt strange to be back in the council wing, but no one's eyes stayed on her long, thanks to the fae glamour. So she let herself slow, taking in the endless row of paintings of officials who had performed their duties for decades, men who had worked with her father when Etta had been barely old enough to swing a sword and women who had children as old as the general and still served alongside the kingsmen they had trained. And others, younger, but still clinging to the traditions of their forebears. Etta stopped, turning to face the wall.

The hall's newest portrait stared down at her with a plaque beneath that read *Gideon Conrad Alexander, Chancellor of Westrende.*

"Conrad," she murmured, thinking of a Lady Conrad she'd

met as a girl. Perhaps the woman had been a ship's captain. Etta could not quite recall, but as she examined the lines of Gideon's face, she felt the hint of recognition at first seeing him fall into place. In the portrait, Gideon wore the same style coat as he'd donned that very morning, and Lord Barrett's depiction of him contained not a single scrap of whimsy. Something dark and determined lurked in the chancellor's eyes, something that spoke of the resolve he meant to put to task. It seemed to swear a vow and proclaim his dourness all at once. Behind Etta, a pair of ladies passed, their eyes skirting hers but their lips turned up at her gawking of the young lord. She paid them no mind, as they could not have known who she truly was. She no longer had a reputation to uphold—not until she broke her fate forsaken curse.

Gideon's figure in the painting was angled not toward the other portraits, but to the empty wall beside it, a bare space where Etta's own portrait should have been.

She walked on, taking each of them in. Her father stared down at her from the greatest height, his shoulders drawn back and his mouth in a hard line. He was proud and stern, holding the bearing of a general, through and through. Etta's mother had said once that it had been difficult for the general to come back from war and have to behave in a civilized manner. Etta wasn't sure one could be civilized and still command such battles. She suspected a person was one or the other and that her father only thrived when there was a war to be fought. Such had certainly been the case in his relationship with Etta.

She let her gaze roam over his coat, the epaulets and trim, a dozen metals of honor. Etta had no metals. Her father had been right—she'd not earned a band marking her as an official of Westrende, but she supposed she'd been in somewhat of a battle, herself, in her four years of training. She had felt strong and capable then, at the top of her class, only to return to the rules her father had set for her and to do as she was told.

Since she was a girl, Etta had been forced to make judgments, to advise and council and possess an opinion on every little matter. It was all part of her training, drilled into her so that she might someday take a post among the kingdom's most powerful. Now, she would not be heard if she screamed from the top of a tower. She was a lowly assistant, an expert in nothing. The chancellor barely trusted her to deliver a letter.

A muttering man passed behind her, and she moved down the wall to stand before the portrait that most touched her. Etta's mother hadn't been especially beautiful in the lines of her face, her figure, or the sheen of her hair, but everyone who knew her instantly became enamored. It was something in the spirit that sprung from her, in the way she tossed her head when she laughed and the sly tilt to her lips as she smiled. When she told a story, the entire hall would fall silent just to hear. She had been made of life. She had positively glowed with it.

The fae had taken that from her. The fae had taken it from all of them.

"They will not take it from me, too," Etta whispered. "Whatever the cost, I will steal it back."

A trio of guards walking by gave notice at her words, and Etta moved on, head down as she strode toward her father's wing.

THE GENERAL'S OFFICE WAS ONE of the most secure areas of the castle. But Etta was the general's daughter and had learned a few of his tricks by mere proximity, having gone through a stage in which she had reveled in uncovering his secrets.

Experience had soured her on the desire to discover things her father kept hidden and on frivolous adventure. But Etta had not forgotten how her father operated. It was little work to find her way outside his chambers, to the narrow space secreted between his office wall and the next. The desire to spy on his visitors had left the general vulnerable to the same, though he would likely suffer an apoplexy, should he discover his own daughter using it against him. Etta waited quietly behind the wall, listening as footsteps came and went, eager for her chance to enter her father's office alone. He had always been a busy man, but the bustle seemed unusually lively, and Etta's intense impatience was tested. In the corner, the shadows seemed to breathe, but Etta held her place.

Inside the office, the door closed again, followed by muffled noises and a pair of booted footfalls. Voices floated through the room—kingsmen, by the sound of them. She leaned against the plaster, her gaze turned away from the darkest corner. Sweat beaded on her temple and beneath the neck of her gown. She did not recall the space being so stifling as girl.

"Already?" a low voice said. "The lady Ostwind has only been missing a day."

Three days, Etta corrected. Surely, the kingsmen Nickolas had said were looking for her had spread word of that. She straightened to shift farther down the wall, her steps light and measured in the dimness, her ears pricked for any movement behind her.

Another voice grumbled, "We can't go on like this, not with this sort of misfortune coming more frequently. It's not just potential kings any longer. What happened with the general's daughter only proves that."

The first man made a grunt of approval. "It's a shame. A

marshal with her disposition is just the sort of enforcement the kingdom needs."

Etta stilled to wonder precisely what he meant. The lightest movement echoed through the space behind her.

Outside, the other man chuckled. "You think her temperament was fitting now, imagine how she would have grown into the post."

Both men's laughter abruptly cut off, followed by the sound of a closing door. In the silence, Etta held her breath. There was a muted string of footfalls, sure and steady, then the nearly imperceptible protest of a chair shifting against the polished marble floor.

"General," the men said in unison. Etta could picture their matching salutes, the way their shoulders tensed with her own, an instinct drilled into them over years.

Her breath was stuck in her chest. She knew she'd held it too long but could not convince herself to release it. She could not fathom what her father had thought of her disappearance or whether he had been laughing it off like the other men. "Only been missing a day," the guard had said. As if it were all a jest to them. As if she'd never returned from training, had not been slated to take place as their marshal, a kingdom official whose rank surpassed their own.

"Report," her father snapped.

There was a shuffling of paper, a short silence, then a slight scrape as her father's chair moved again. "Unacceptable. Get out of my sight with this. If I see you again before she is found—"

He did not need to finish the order. He'd likely not even stood. Heavy footsteps hurried from the room, the two who'd been laughing and an apparent third kingsman, whom Etta had not heard speak at all. She was grateful she'd not had a chance to attempt entry, because the silent man would have seen her caught.

The door closed, and there was a soft sound as something settled onto the desk. His hand, perhaps. It was too hot inside the space, too narrow. The shadows were too close. She leaned against the wall, pressing her palm to the dusty plaster. She could only picture him, alone at his desk, just paces away from the thin panel she hid behind and from a truth he refused to acknowledge, that remaining silent could not keep the fae from hurting them.

Her father sighed, the sound a knife to Etta's resolve. She had meant to wait for him to leave, to steal the book that would help her cross the wall. To do it all on her own. To face the fae. But he had an army of men at his command, a kingdom that might be able to save her... if he would only let them.

Etta's heart was in her throat, hot and hammering and preventing even a swallow. He had sent her away. *I would send you off for another four if I could.* But when she came back, he'd let her stay and stand before council. She was the one who had failed. And now, she was missing. His daughter was gone, nothing in her place but the body of the man who'd been hired to paint her. He might have thought Etta was responsible, that she'd killed Lord Barrett and run off to save her skin. Or worse, that she'd been stolen, taken by the fae for the sin of speaking their name.

Taken, as Etta's mother had been. Seized by the prince of the fae.

It was her fault, he would assume. If only she had behaved and done as she'd been told.

Her father didn't have the sight, but he knew the truth about magic. He understood there were fae who crossed into Westrende. If anyone would know her, if anyone could truly see...

A strip of light cut through the darkness as Etta's slick

palm pressed the secret panel open before she'd had time to think it through.

She realized her mistake in an instant.

SOMETHING CHITTERED in the darkness beside her. In the room beyond the doorway, General Ostwind was standing, sword in hand, before Etta had even a moment to speak.

"To the floor!" he ordered, her father no longer. His was the voice of a man trained in battle and who would make no hesitation in cutting her in two.

"Father," she said anyway, "it's me."

He was moving toward her, as agile as any beast, his grip sure on the sword.

Etta held her hands forward in surrender. "Please. Just listen."

The tip of his sword cut off her plea. It pressed to her neck in one smooth gesture, only the brief flash of metal catching her eye before a trickle of warm blood slid down her skin. She'd not yet felt its sting.

"Who sent you?" he asked in a low voice, offering a warning. He'd no need to call the guard, not with his blade at her throat. The gesture showed he intended to kill her, just as clearly as any word he might have said. He did not need a witness to slay an intruder. Not as a general.

"It's me," she choked out. "Etta."

Her voice had not changed—surely, he could at least know that. But his eyes were cold, bearing no hint of recognition. His weapon remained steady. "You dare speak her name."

The fae, she wanted to scream at him. *The fae did this.* But Etta could not. The last thing her father would accept would have been the invoking of them by a stranger, a girl with an unfamiliar face.

"Don't believe what you see," she begged.

He stepped forward, his blade digging deeper. *Last chance*, the gesture warned.

"Yes," she answered aloud, because Etta knew it was true. She'd been a fool to ever believe he might listen or to think that her disappearance would mean enough to change things. One more word, no matter what it was, would be her last. So she moved slowly, easing the necklace from the pocket of her skirt. She held it forward, letting the chain that held her mother's locket drop from her open palm at his eye level, because a man like the general would never look away from an opponent, should she have tossed it.

The flinch didn't show on his face, but Etta felt it through the tip of his sword. It was her one opportunity. Her only opening.

She rolled backward, away from her father and into the narrow space from which she'd come. He was on her in a moment, but from the darkness shot the ball of dark fur that had been watching her all along. It pounced at the general, drawn by her blood, and that single moment of hesitation was all Etta needed to land a hand on the panel to her escape. The general's curse echoed off the walls behind her, but she didn't waste time by closing the door or attempting to shove furniture in front of it. She needed only three paces, three good steps toward the next doorway, and she'd be in the hidden walkways used by staff.

He would never find her, not with a maze of options from which to choose. Etta burst through the doorway and slammed bodily into a woman a solid head taller than her. A huff of breath escaped them both, then Etta was up, tumbling forward though a passage at random, not precisely to her plan. Behind her, she heard the woman spluttering an explanation to Etta's father, but the thunder of his chasing foot-steps never came. Etta could not wait around to discover why. He'd had no change of heart, despite that she had handed over her mother's token, she was sure of that. More likely, he'd only decided not to chase after her like a fool.

He would tell his kingsmen, put them on alert. He would not have accounted for the glamour on her face, the way it would turn a man's gaze no matter how he tried. In truth, her father may have forgotten already the very details he would need to identify his intruder.

She would not be grateful to the curse, even for that. Etta flung herself through the next doorway, pressed the panel closed behind her, and leaned against its wood. Chest heav-ing, hands slick, she pulled the kerchief from her pocket to wipe at the blood streaking her neck. The wound hurt but not badly. There was something to be said for a sharp blade. But it smeared, already thick, and she counted herself fortu-nate to have landed in an empty study. She found a decanter, poured water over the kerchief, then drew a chair out before the small writing desk to pen a message of her own.

If her father refused to see her for who she truly was, then she would act as herself in the only way she could.

CHAPTER 12

Bloodied and sweating, Etta had taken the letter for her father to Nickolas, who'd been entirely put out by her reappearance, let alone that she'd ordered him to deliver a message to the very man who might implicate him in a crime. But he had eventually agreed, and Etta had returned to the chancery's wing in time for a meal, a bath, an hour's research to catch up on the task Gideon had set for the marshal, and a solid night's sleep. All should have been well by the next morning, except that in a fresh gown, standing beside the chancellor as he examined a parchment clearly not meant for his eyes, Etta was starting to suspect more than the fates were playing against her.

The script on the letter she'd had delivered—not to the chancellor but to her father—was entirely her own, the signature intact. No one could have disputed that. But clearly, someone had. Gideon's desk was spread with documents Etta had signed years before, personal correspondence and public contracts. His expert chancellor's gaze traced the lines, studying their curves as he held each beside the one she'd penned just the night before, yet he did not seem convinced.

Etta had eased closer through the morning, finding reasons to sort and file ever nearer to his desk.

Finally, she broke. "You think it is not her? That someone delivered a forgery?"

Gideon's head snapped up, and Etta realized she had leaned more closely than a mere assistant ought. She caught the scent of him, that hint of woodruff and soap, but it tangled with something else, familiar and warm. The scent was her own, she realized, the parchment in his hand having come freshly out of the possessions in her trunk. He slid the documents into a single pile, apparently assuming she was interested in gathering gossip to trade among castle staff. It was better, she supposed, than having him think she was sniffing his person.

She straightened. "It's only that it seems unlike the lady Ostwind, from what I've heard. What would she gain from bludgeoning a poor artist to death? He was to make her portrait, after all. And the years of work she'd put toward becoming marshal... it makes no sense that she'd throw it all away without reason."

Gideon's lips pressed closed. "That is not for me to judge. But a single message does not clear her name, not when it was first in the hands of her father."

"Her father? You believe him—what? That he somehow may be covering for her? You truly think so badly of the general and his kin?"

Gideon pushed away from the desk to stand, the documents—her documents—pressed to his chest in the way he'd held a stack of parchment the first time she'd seen him. But the man could not have been mistaken for a simple clerk any longer, not by the manner he carried himself or his tone.

"Continue the filing, my lady. I've a few errands to tend to. I'll send Jules in to assist you."

It was a reminder of her place. He'd given her a position as his assistant, and the business of Westrende was not hers to weigh. Gideon didn't trust her alone in his office. The chancery did need to remain secure, but Etta was part of its staff.

She didn't know why she'd expected him to trust her as his assistant when he hadn't trusted her as Lady Ostwind, but it rankled her. He thought Etta's letter was a fake, that she was a fraud who had kingdom officials lying for her. Etta's father was the general, head of council. She didn't know what more the man wanted. It was fine, then. If Gideon needed more than a letter passed to General Ostwind, she would give him one from Antonetta Ostwind herself.

"My lady?"

Etta glanced up to find Jules in the doorway, her focus on the crumpled document in Etta's hand. Etta cleared her throat and offered a weak smile. "Just keeping up with this filing."

It took her most of the afternoon to get away long enough to write a few measly words, not counting the quarter hour she'd spent attempting to locate parchment that would not give her ruse away. The chancellor had proven he would inspect whatever she sent him to the finest detail, so paper pulled from his own supply would never do. When she finally had it folded and ready to leave on his desk, she became aware of another issue: no one in the office would be able to attest to how the missive had been delivered.

Her savior came in the form of Nickolas Brigham.

"My lady," Robert said from the doorway. "Lord Brigham is requesting a word with you. He insisted that he not reveal his name, but everyone knows who he is." He pushed a piece of sandy hair from his brow. "Shall I send him away?"

Etta blinked up at the boy from her sorting. "No, thank you. I'll take care of it myself." As she stood, brushing her skirts, Jules gave her a speculative glance. "All's well," Etta promised. "He's a friend of the family." Then she hurried from the room before she had to invent an entire battalion of relatives to befriend the man.

Nickolas lingered in the shadows outside the entrance to the chancery's office, glancing about as if involved in something illicit.

"What are you doing here?" she hissed, taking hold of his sleeve to pull him farther from the doorway. "You're the one who insisted we reveal no ties to one another."

"The letter to your father didn't work," he snapped. "No one believes it's real. Furthermore, the fact that a missing person sent a message at all is suspect. This does not look good, Etta, and you should know that once they've ruled you out for being too missing to blame, I'm the next closest witness to a man's death."

"Quit being a coward." At his outraged expression, she stepped nearer. "I know the letter didn't work. The chancellor himself was tasked with verifying it. But I have a new plan that will buy us both time."

His eyes narrowed. "Why do I not like the sound of this?"

"Because I need you to deliver it."

He leaned closer and kept his voice low. "I may owe you, Antonetta, but not so much as this."

"It's this or an investigation into your private dealings by the entire office of marshal. Which do you prefer?"

Something that sounded like a curse ground out of him, just as movement caught the corner of her eye. Gideon was crossing through the corridor on his way to the chancery entrance. He met her gaze.

"Margaretta, a word, please."

She swallowed, taking a step back from Nickolas before giving Gideon a small nod that she hoped he understood meant she would be along shortly.

"Margaretta?" Nickolas murmured.

Etta rammed an elbow into his stomach, watching until Gideon was out of sight. Then she turned. "I cannot very well claim to be Antonetta, can I?" He opened his mouth, likely to remind her it was not the name but the familiarity he was pointing out, and she shoved the letter into his hand. "Get this delivered. As soon as possible."

"Must you keep tangling me in your—"

"You are all I have," she said in a harsh whisper. "The fae stole the face of the general's daughter right beneath the council's watch, and no one will even acknowledge their existence. It's up to me to fix this. The only way I ever will is if I break this curse and become marshal of Westrende. I have to, Nickolas. And the only help I have is you, whether either of us likes it."

Etta did not wait for his reply, but his words at her back stopped her cold. She'd barely gone three steps.

"They're replacing the marshal. Council had a special meeting this afternoon. They sent Lord Alexander the letter that was addressed to your father, and he would not confirm its authenticity. With you missing and another prospect for king taken ill..." His words fell off, but Etta could not make herself look at him. "That's why I've come. At the turn of the moon, a new marshal will step into the post, whether or not you have cleared your name."

"Thank you for telling me. I-I appreciate what you've done, Nickolas, and the risk. I won't ask anything more of you aside from the letters."

Her heart heavy, Etta forced her feet to carry her forward. She did not look back. Whatever Nickolas thought, whatever her father and council did, it would not change the outcome. Westrende's marshal was the one person who could stop the fae. If Etta ever meant to succeed, it had to be her. She owed it to her mother. She owed it to the kingdom.

When she came back into the chancellor's office, Gideon

was not sitting at his desk. He was leaned against the front edge of it, arms folded over his chest, his expression grim. She had quite forgotten he'd caught her in the corridor with Nickolas. He tilted his chin toward a chair that waited across from him.

Etta crossed the space slowly then sat. "My lord."

He stared down at her. "As chancellor, my reputation rests on the shoulders of those associated with this office. My duty is to uphold the sanctity of law and ensure justice is carried out in every instance so that the kingdom remains safe and its people prosper."

It was difficult to keep the frown from her face, but despite the effect of the glamour, Gideon's focus on her facade did not waver, so Etta managed. He uncrossed his arms. "As such, we all risk a great deal when a new member of staff is taken on. For it is not only my reputation that might pay the price for a poor venture. It is the entire staff of this office, every soul you have and have not yet met who has found a place within these walls."

"My lord?"

Gideon reached behind him to retrieve a crumpled parchment from his desk. He held it forward, and in the light, Etta could see that its edge was smeared dark, a color that Gideon might not recognize as day-old blood.

The exchequer's message.

He clearly took note of the realization sinking in, as Etta recalled that instead of delivering it as she'd promised she would, she had not. He couldn't have known that she'd snuck into her father's office instead, been chased through the staff passageways, and delivered her own missive to Nickolas's rooms. But she could not believe she had forgotten the reason she'd been let out of his sight in the first place.

Gideon dropped the letter back to his desk. "I cannot in

good faith keep someone on staff who cannot be trusted, Margaretta."

Saints, he did not know the half of it. Even the name was a lie. "Please," she started, but Gideon left her no room.

He sighed, turning from her to round his desk. "It is not my place to warn you of personal matters, my lady, but I feel I should not leave it unsaid." He sat, drawing his chair forward to position himself in the most officious manner he might, plainly uncomfortable at what he intended not to leave unsaid. "The"—he stopped then started again, and Etta realized the word he'd abandoned was "gentleman"—"the *lord* with whom you were meeting outside—"

Etta stood so abruptly that it startled them both. Wherever the cool calm had gone from her years of training, she could not find it. "You cannot dismiss me. You mustn't. It was only a misunderstanding. I truly was on my way to deliver the letter when—I was—I had an accident, and there was—" She stepped forward. "Lord Brigham is only a family friend. He notified me of-of the accident, and—" Her hands found his desk, clinging in a way she would not be proud of when she looked back on it later. "Please do not dismiss me. I need this post more than you could possibly understand."

Gideon had gone silent, his expression blank. He stared at her with such open expressionlessness that she had no idea what his next words might be.

"Please," she begged. "There's nowhere else for me." *Let me stay.*

"My lord." Jules's voice rang from outside the doorway, breaking the tension so thoroughly that Etta jumped.

His gaze was on hers only a moment longer before he glanced at the door. "Yes?"

Jules's face popped into view. "I have those documents you —" She looked from Gideon to Etta. "Oh, I apologize if I've interrupted."

"No." Gideon cleared his throat. "Just leave the documents here, Jules. Thank you. And, if you will, won't you take Margaretta to the archives so that she might help your search for the records of the Richards plea."

THE NEXT MORNING, Etta was up well before dawn. Jules lay sprawled on the bunk opposite, limbs akimbo, braid slung across her face, and one booted foot wedged between the mattress and wall. Beneath the drape of its cage, the bird purred. Etta had mended her borrowed gown the night before and hurriedly slid into it so that she might have time to find more current records of the prospects for king and Gideon's task. Time was spending faster than she had imagined possible, and it was getting no easier to live the life of someone else.

She needed to complete a report that would prove to council, if not to Gideon himself, that Lady Ostwind was up to the post of marshal, steal back into her father's office to retrieve his book, and get over the wall to win back her face.

Her forehead thunked against the door at the very thought of all that standing between her and success, but Etta took a deep breath, tightened the tie of her dress, and opened the door to leave the room.

She'd nearly waited too long to retrieve the records of the incidents involving the prospects for king and the various investigations, but Gideon had given her a second—*third?*—chance. She would not waste it. At least if she had possession of the records, being thrown out of chancery would not hurt quite so badly.

The clerk's desk was empty, no one in the entire office moving besides a humming Tobias tucked away in the stacks of a back room, as he so often was. Jules had explained that Tobias sometimes took ill, so when he felt well, he caught up on work, whether night or day. *As long as he's out of the way, it doesn't bother anyone,* Jules had noted in a tone that made clear it wasn't to bother Etta. It hadn't, but Etta was beginning to appreciate the uncommon protectiveness among the chancery staff.

By the time she was able to locate where the reports should have been, only to find the space empty, the others had stirred, and Robert began heating the water for morning tea. Etta had no idea when Jules might let her out of her sight again, but she was forced to end her search before she was caught. Tidying her skirts, she made her way into the chancellor's office so it might appear she'd been working only on the task of sorting.

Gideon had not yet arrived. She walked quietly around his desk, sliding open two drawers to nothing of interest before finding a third locked. It was the contents of the fourth drawer that stopped her cold, the narrowest one and closest to his seat. Beneath a few folded documents rested a missive she recognized as her own. A ribbon of the lightest blue clung to the broken wax seal of the house of one of her oldest friends. The girl had been shipped away to another kingdom, well before Etta had gone off to a separate kingdom for her own training. Her father had refused to let Etta visit, and once she'd left Westrende, their messages had been fewer and farther between.

The only letter from her they might have found when searching Etta's rooms would have been the one stashed in her traveling trunk. She'd held onto the message because it had been one of the last and because it had spoken of the dedication Etta had shown and how proud Etta's mother would have been. *Taken,* the message had said. Taken from Etta in a manner far too cruel.

Etta had wondered about the wording of the letter and whether leaving the kingdom had allowed her friend to accept the truths of Westrende. She had not asked, though, because she'd feared the answer might be no, that the reference had only meant taken from the world while unfairly young.

The drawer slid quietly closed beneath Etta's palm. Gideon had received her personal correspondence in the line of duty. Etta could claim no such excuse. She was not marshal yet, and had she been, Gideon was not the man she was meant to be investigating.

He'd given her a reprieve and let her stay on at the chancery, but he hadn't trusted her enough to leave her alone, so she would not riffle through the rest of his things, even if it was tempting. Getting caught would have been the end of her access to the entire wing.

Instead, she drew her chair toward the endless stack of documents she was meant to sort and file, but before she settled in, she heard a muffled sound from beyond the far shelf of books. Etta glanced toward the empty office door then at the hint of dawn light visible through the high windows.

The sound came again.

She stood, smoothed her skirt, then crossed to the shelf of books. It rose tall, overflowing with bound volumes, its wood thick and dark. Behind it waited more shelves, just as sturdy, making a maze of sorts that led to the office's far wall. Etta should have turned back, but another dense thud sounded in the room beyond, followed by a low grunt.

She moved through the darkness, her hand on the lever before she could talk sense into it. The door slid open to reveal a large, nearly empty room. A few scattered candles burned unsteadily on untrimmed wicks, lighting the space enough to reveal that a small number of furnishings had been slid to the outer walls and a bare wood floor, worn with age. A lean figure clad in trousers and shirtsleeves centered the room. He moved with the ease of a practiced swordsman —*step, swing, back, spin, thrust*—just as Etta had done for years. But there was no master swordsman battering him with a rod, no sparring partner taunting his swings. Only Gideon, alone, his blade polished and grip steady, the flash of metal mesmerizing as he moved. Beyond him waited a post and dummies, apparently the source of the muffled thuds.

Etta could not draw her eyes from Gideon, though she knew she should. Jules had said the chancellor had private business to attend each morning, but this was not what Etta had expected. Hair tousled, temples damp with sweat, the buttoned-up man she'd come to loathe was gone. Even the laces of his shirt were undone halfway down his chest. Beneath the thin fabric was lean muscle, shifting with every graceful strike. He moved through the room at a steady pace, his form that of someone who had been practicing even longer than Etta. He tossed the blade from one hand to the other, and the motion that followed was nearly as smooth. The turn of his blade took him partially out of her view, and Etta inched forward to see.

Her shoulder bumped a garment rack by the doorway, and something metal fell from its coat to clatter to the floor. Etta froze. Gideon's head snapped in her direction, his stunned gaze cutting into hers for one long moment before his expression shifted.

"I was... I just—" was all she managed before a wet, hairy beast knocked her to the floor.

CHAPTER 13

"Clara!" Gideon yelled, his footsteps pounding ever nearer as Etta tried to roll away from the dog. By the wall, the thing was unbelievably massive. It had to have had too much fur.

Etta had only half a moment to consider whether a dog could possess less fur without being more offensive before the clamoring beast was hauled off her.

"Down," Gideon commanded. The creature was led to another room, and Gideon was back at Etta's side, kneeling with a hand out, presumably to help her to her feet.

Flicking her hands vigorously, Etta moaned. "Why is she so wet?"

Gideon's mouth pressed together as he made a sound of what might have been chagrin but that could not be ruled out as a repressed laugh.

Etta narrowed her gaze at him, just in case.

If it had been humor, he managed a sober enough reply. "We go for a morning swim."

"We?" Etta asked, horrified.

He did smile then, if just a little. His face wasn't perfect, she realized. Up close, she could see that the bridge of his nose bore a small crook, as if it might have once been broken. And there, by the corner of his eye, was a tiny white scar, faint with age. His lips... no, they were perfect.

"We go," he said. "Clara swims."

"And then you practice swords. Every morning."

A hint of color rose to his cheeks. "Are you injured, my lady?"

Etta glanced down at herself, her fresh dress littered with hunks of wet fur. "I—" She looked back at him, too close, too concerned. He did not know who she was, not truly. But something in Gideon's gaze said that he saw her, that even if his eyes did not linger on her face, they connected with hers, the only recognizable part of Lady Ostwind that remained. "I wanted to say thank you for yesterday. And I-I only meant to get an early start."

Her voice was soft enough to encompass both shame and an apology, and Gideon simply nodded before he reached for her dog-dampened hand. He pulled her with him to stand. "It's early enough, indeed. You've time to run back and change into a fresh dress if you'd like."

Etta sighed. "I've only the two. Better make do as is."

His brow drew down. "I'll have the clerk issue your payment this week. You've done a few days' work already, and I'm certain he'll release just that if nothing else."

"Oh, I don't mean to make trouble. I've done quite enough of that already. I'll just wash up and let you get back to..." She glanced at the open space across the room where he'd been practicing.

"What?" Gideon asked softly.

She met his gaze, direct and sure, the way she might have done as Antonetta Ostwind. "Would you like a partner to spar with, my lord?"

OFFERING to spar with Gideon had been the most advantageous move Etta could have made. He'd been stiff at first, too careful, and she wasn't normally one for showing off, but it was clear he would not lean into the match until she'd proven her skill. One quick move had his sword batted aside as she sprang forward into his space, the tip of her own weapon hovering threateningly near the soft bits beneath his ear. His eyes widened almost imperceptibly when he realized he would have to back away to ready another strike. Etta did not give him the chance. She spun, pressed, and struck again, keeping him on the defense until he was backed against the dummy.

"My lady," he said mildly, "it appears I've underestimated your ability."

"That can be forgiven," Etta said, "as long as you hold back no longer."

The hint of a smile crossed his lips before he moved for her, and something in Etta's belly flipped. He was quick. Precise. A match to Etta in agility. But he had her in speed.

His technique was confined by his training, but Etta had learned countless fighting styles to prepare for the post as marshal. She relaxed into the motions of a style that fit his, and soon, it was as if they'd practiced together for years. Gideon seemed truly to be enjoying himself.

Etta relished it, too, the muscles she'd not used for days as she'd sat hunched over documents in a thinly padded chair, sighing with relief at finally being able to move. Nickolas had refused to spar with her on their journey despite his fancy sword, citing a fear of being trounced in front of the king's guard, but Etta suspected it had been more because she was the general's daughter. A misstep might have meant something different when a man had to answer to the head of council.

But Gideon had no idea. She was only Margaretta to him, a new assistant who seemed unnaturally skilled with a blade. And once he had warmed to her, his guard began to come down, the staid expressions and steady posture a show put on for all of Westrende. If she were to guess, he'd had to so the council and the others would take him more seriously. Because Gideon, it turned out, had quite the boyish grin.

"No," he said with a laugh at Etta's stories. "It cannot be true."

"It is. I swear by it, my lord. To this day, I cannot heft a sword without recalling the sound of that costermonger's oath as his fruit tumbled streetward at the hands of a girl no more than four. My first and only criminal act. I was given a tutor the same afternoon and warned that if I meant to wield a sword, I would without question know how to use it."

"My lady, I would never have guessed." Gideon drew his sword back, coming to rest as he shook his head.

Etta chuckled, flipping hers so that she might offer him the grip. "Enough for today?"

"Indeed. For there is much to be done." His eyes remained on her a moment longer, then he came forward, taking possession of the weapon before moving to stow them both away.

"And what are we working on this morning?" she asked as casually as she might manage.

The levity fell from Gideon's being. "Nothing so enjoyable as this."

Etta stepped closer. "Is it Lady Ostwind? Have they discovered where she might be?"

"No." He ran a palm up the back of his neck. "In fact, the entire ordeal has become more complicated."

Etta could not have stopped her sharp gaze if she'd wanted to, but she kept her voice low. "How so?"

Gideon's lips pulled down in a true frown that felt entirely appropriate as he picked up his chancellor's shirt. He glanced at her then gestured vaguely with the garment as he stepped behind a screen. Etta waited impatiently. One arm and a bit of his shoulder stuck out from behind the partition as he drew the thin white shirt over his head and tossed it aside. The muscles of his back shifted as he leaned forward to grab the fresh one, and an unexpected flush of heat shot through her at the sight of lean muscle flexing beneath bare skin. But the clean shirt was one of the slim black versions that he wore as chancellor, and she forced herself to look away.

Behind the partition, Gideon said, "This morning I received another letter, directly from the Lady Ostwind herself."

"So it's true," Etta said breathily in mock surprise, thinking that Nickolas had taken his time in delivering the letter. "She's really out there?"

Gideon stepped out to face her, still fastening the shirt at his neck. "I can't be sure. But the message says that she is performing her duty to the kingdom."

"Her duty?" Etta prompted, unable to let his consistent disbelief go unchallenged. Two letters from the lady herself. She didn't know what more the man could need—perhaps a vow before a king or a contract signed in blood.

"She claims to be hunting Lord Barrett's killer and says that she will prove her innocence when she returns."

"So she's coming back. Thank the fates. You should send a note to council. They'll want to cancel their plans to replace the marshal, posthaste."

His gaze cut to hers.

"Because she's coming back," Etta explained.

"We shouldn't be discussing this, my lady. Best we return to work. The both of us."

"But she must have the chance. If she can prove that it wasn't her, that all along she was pursuing justice, then she possesses just the sort of character the office of marshal requires."

Gideon's palm slid over his chest as if the very idea pained him, though perhaps he was only straightening his shirt. Perhaps Etta was spending far too much time examining his expressions and following his hands and attempting to force him to see the issues from a side he so adamantly refused to. Perhaps she should have knocked him out with a sleeping draft and spent the morning rummaging his files in search of the reports she needed.

Certainly, she should stop having thoughts of both kinds, unfit as they were for a marshal.

"If she returns, if she completes her task satisfactorily, then all will have been done fairly. I will stand by my word." He gave her one final look before gesturing toward the door. "You can trust in that, my lady, if nothing else."

Etta followed, forcing whatever else she might have said to stay on her tongue. The events of the last fortnight had thrown her off balance, and she'd forgotten her training. Fear had driven her to disobey her father's orders and return home early, and anger had seen her caught half-dressed in a public corridor with Nickolas. Emotion had failed her in her encounters with council, with Gideon, and with the fae who had set a curse upon her. She knew how best to play the situation to her advantage.

It was time she did so.

Gideon paused at the doorway to remove his officer's coat from the garment rack, and Etta glanced down at the bit of metal that had fallen earlier as it flashed on the floor. It was a signet ring, gold and garnet, and as she bent to scoop it up, she realized it did not belong to the chancellor of Westrende, despite that it had escaped a pocket of his coat.

Gideon glanced back at her, and she tucked the ring inside her boot, pretending to secure the lace. "Ready?" she asked, coming to stand just as he pulled the lever.

"I'll be right in," he told her. "I only need a moment to release Clara from her prison."

Etta gave him a look. "You say that as if she has not committed a crime against my person."

Gideon bowed his head, a hint of the smile he'd worn that morning flashing over his lips. "She seems particularly fond of crimes against your person, my lady."

Etta stepped closer. "An incident that does not need repeated to Jules, I trust."

His hand moved solemnly to his heart. "You have my vow."

CHAPTER 14

The door came open to a frowning Jules, arms crossed over her chest and eyes on her employer.

"Jules," Gideon said. "Good morning."

Her gaze moved purposely to Etta. "Is it? I wouldn't know because I've spent the last hour looking for..." Her words trailed off as she took in the state of Etta's hair and her fur-spotted dress. "I just had this washed."

Etta winced. "I'll clean the mess myself. It's not your burden."

Jules uncrossed her arms then reached past Gideon to drag Etta through. "It's not the burden I'm concerned about. It's the reputation of this office." She threw a glare over her shoulder at Gideon. "And what might happen to poor Clara if anyone realizes there's a dog terrorizing the entire wing."

At the sound of Jules's condemnation, a muffled whine came from behind the other door. But Etta was led to a small storage room, where she could brush fur from the front of her gown with a tool Jules apparently kept at the ready. Before the woman had a chance to scold Etta for taking off unannounced and interrupting the chancellor's morning routine,

Robert came searching for Jules, and Etta was set to task with more busywork and a warning that Jules would quickly return.

The morning carried on much the same, and eventually, Etta glanced up from her documents to realize that the last time Jules had hovered nearby with an eye on her was much longer than it should have been. She stood, stretching her legs, then crept into the storage room to which Jules had disappeared, only to find it dark. Inching forward, she pressed the door wider to let in light from the next room. Tucked neatly between the shelves on a small, padded seat, Jules's petite from was curled so that her head rested against her knees, her back and boots holding her upright as she appeared to sleep. Etta stared for a moment, unsure, but a deep, easy breath lifted the woman's shoulders, so Etta eased out of the room.

Closing the door carefully behind her, Etta glanced about the main chamber. She'd been left alone, finally, for whatever brief span of time it might be. She did not waste it. Scouring the crates and cabinets, Etta searched for any sign at all of the investigations into the prospects for king. Not a single document was present in any of the places she might have expected, and when Jules—appearing as if she'd not just been taking a midmorning nap—returned from the storeroom to check her progress, Etta—appearing as if she'd not just ransacked the room—inquired about the filing system in any way she could.

The day passed with no progress in the matter, though, and Etta was beginning to suspect that the reports were locked somewhere she would not have access to. She was itching for progress in any matter, especially given how difficult it would be to return to her father's office since he'd caught her—or rather, Margaretta—behind his walls. When night fell, the chancery staff sleeping soundly with it, Etta could not seem to lie still in the narrow bunk of their dark room. She dressed quietly then sneaked into one of the smaller offices, where the castle guards might not catch her moving about after hours. Climbing onto the wide ledge of a window, she leaned against its cool glass and tucked her legs close to her chest. The night sky stared back at her, a sliver of moon warning that time was running out.

She'd wasted too many days already, days she could never get back. Whatever game the fae were playing, Etta's chances of saving herself were slipping from her grasp. She tugged the ring from the hidden pouch at her waist, twisting it in the dim light. It had fallen from a pocket of the chancellor's coat, she was sure. And yet she could not for the life of her understand why. Gideon had dealings with her father's office—a chancellor would sign and verify and file any number of documents a general and the council might need. But to have possession of another man's ring, a man who was head of the council and important to the kingdom... Etta could not make it make sense.

Without question, the ring belonged to her father. It had his colors, his insignia, and was a piece he'd worn for years. The general's name might as well have been inscribed upon it. How it had ended up among Gideon's things was a mystery.

Etta slid the thing over her thumb, unable to stop herself from thinking about the mystery that was Gideon. He'd been so stiff and formal every moment she'd worked across from his desk. But at play, Gideon had moved with easy grace, his eyes lighting with laughter, his usually stern mouth soft in a smile.

He didn't know this Margaretta well enough to trust her. He and Jules had barely left her alone since she'd come on staff. But when she'd stood with him after their swordplay, he'd confessed details about the lady Ostwind that made clear he was conflicted about giving Etta a chance. Why a stranger might have warranted repeated chances when someone well

known in the kingdom did not should have been plain—
because as he'd said, a marshal must be above reproach. But it
felt like something more. It felt as if he'd not trusted her even
before she'd returned.

Never mind that she had vowed to crush him before
they'd even met. Whatever she was, Gideon was not. He was
as straight-laced and by the book as they came.

Except for the ring.

Her finger idly spun the metal over her thumb, the
starlight winking out as clouds moved overhead. Maybe she
had been mistaken. But Gideon was entirely by the book—at
least that much, she was certain of. She would have to
complete his task by the next moon, as he had vowed. And
he, trustworthy and loyal chancellor that he was, would have
documents of such importance secreted away, where he would
not have to worry about who he could trust not to find them.
Etta needed a better way to retrieve the reports.

And she had just the plan to make it work.

A muffled *whuff* sounded from through the glass, and Etta
glanced toward the courtyard. Among the shrubbery, Clara
bounced, limned in moonlight as she darted to and fro,
sniffing various topiaries before circling the choicest land-
scape. Beyond her, near the overhang of an upper-floor
balcony, stood Gideon in his most drab robe. His hair was
wild, his posture resigned, and he looked on at that horrible
dog with nothing but devotion. She had to fight the smile
that tugged at her lips.

"My lady."

The voice jolted Etta from her reverie, and she shoved the
ring into her pocket as she turned. The voice belonged to a
kingsman, one of the guards set to patrol the castle corridors
in the chancery wing. The kingsman would report directly to
Gideon.

"Best not to wander this late," he told her, his gaze moving slowly from Etta to the scene outside.

Etta stood, brushing a hand now empty of her father's ring over her skirts. "Of course. I'll get back to my rooms. Couldn't sleep, is all."

"Aye," he said. "Takes a bit to become accustomed to a new place. But you'll find your rhythm soon and settle in for the long years."

Etta could only hope not, but she gave him a smile then slid a piece of blank parchment off a side table on her way out of the room.

EARLY THE NEXT MORNING, Etta slipped the letter for Gideon in among a pile of others Robert had retrieved at dawn. Jules had returned her to Gideon's office to continue sorting the crates she'd started on her first day, under Gideon's supervision. When he opened the message, he made a strange sound that Etta assumed was an intake of breath, but she dared not look up, lest her expression give her away.

He stood, pushing back from his desk then crossing to the door. "Robert," he called. "Where did you pick up this missive?"

Robert came closer to examine the letter, mumbled something about not recalling seeing it at all, then apologized profusely. Gideon disappeared into the main office for what must have been a quarter hour before he finally returned. He strode to his desk with such purpose that Etta let herself look up with an attempt at concern.

Gideon sat heavily, elbow resting beside the stack of unfolded messages, fingers woven helplessly through a mess of hair. His other hand pressed Lady Ostwind's letter flat, his gaze pinned to her words.

It was a request for the records she required in order to complete his task. A demand, more precisely, that he deliver them to her assistant by the authority granted her by council and kingdom. It had been written carefully in her own hand, signed by her full name, and sealed with the emblem from her father's ring.

It felt a little cruel to have done it as she watched from her seat across the room. But he'd left her with little choice. She stood. "My lord, is something amiss?"

Gideon raised his face to look at her.

"Is there anything I can do?"

He shook his head. Etta moved closer. He folded the parchment and slid it aside, though she did not miss that it became determinedly pinned by his elbow. The document that had rested beneath it on the stack was a standard recognition of title, nothing worthy of the look Gideon was giving it. His other hand smoothed his hair back into place with a single swipe.

"Thank you," he said. "But you're free to take the afternoon to assist Jules or..." He glanced up at her again. "You say—"

Etta stepped forward, only the desk between them. "What is it?"

Gideon's gaze slid briefly to the door. "You say that Lord Brigham is a family friend."

"Yes." Etta shrugged. "Can't be helped, I'm afraid."

He did not laugh.

Etta pursed her lips. "Is there something you need, in regard to Nickolas?"

"How well do you know him?"

"Well enough to know that he's mostly harmless, whatever your assumptions."

Gideon's shoulders straightened. "Right. My apologies, Margaretta. I meant no insult to you or your family by voicing my concerns before."

Etta waved him off. "It's true, he has no sense of propriety when there's someone he means to charm. But his intent is rarely ill, and he has a good heart somewhere in there."

"I shouldn't pry."

"My lord, tell me what it is that you want to know."

Gideon sighed, leaning back in his chair to take the letter from Etta in hand. The parchment slid between his fingers as he spoke, his expression grave. "Can he be trusted?"

CHAPTER 15

Nickolas could not be trusted with state secrets, but Etta hadn't been about to confess that when he was the only ally she had. Instead, she'd convinced Gideon to deliver a set of highly confidential reports regarding the prospects for king, as the Lady Ostwind had demanded. And so, on Margaretta's day off, she sat on a chaise in Nickolas's suite, pouring through reports while the rake of ill repute paced nervously before her.

"You said the letters were all. You said you'd involve me no further."

She did not look up, as they'd been having the same conversation for the past hour. "You're not involved. I just need your suite for a few hours. Leave if you want. Go out with that pack of beasts you call friends."

He flopped onto the chair opposite her. "I call you a friend. And here, you're the beastliest of all."

Etta had fallen silent in her reading, and Nickolas sat up. "Antonetta," he said. "What's wrong?"

Her face had gone pale, she knew, but she couldn't manage to play it off as nothing. She'd paged through dozens of reports, accounts of how and when the prospects had fallen ill, been involved in regrettable accidents, and suffered a host of general misfortunes. But suddenly, the investigation had taken an unexpected turn in the form of an unlikely connection to a single individual.

Etta met Nickolas's gaze. "What do you know of the prospects for king? The investigations."

He shrugged. "Only rumor, and a bit about the interviews. My mother and that lord—what was his name? Richard? Randolf?" He shook his head. "The marshal had called them in to inquire whether they'd witnessed anything suspect at the winter ball."

"The ball?"

Nickolas leaned forward, his elbows resting on his knees and his fingers laced. "Yes. The eldest of the prospects had taken ill that night. Apparently, no one else had symptoms of anything outside of a bit too much punch."

"You were there?"

"Of course. I go every year. Wouldn't miss it."

She wet her lips. Took a breath.

"Etta?"

She stared at him, hating that she had to ask. "Was my father present?"

Nickolas's brow shifted. "I don't—yes, I suppose. He usually is."

"You've heard nothing else?"

"Saints, what is it? The face you're wearing is utterly—" His words cut off at the realization that the face she was wearing was not hers at all. His voice dropped. "Your expression, is all. I meant your expression."

"Paper," she demanded. "And your best quill and ink."

Nickolas gestured toward the writing desk against the wall, a grand station that appeared to be little used. "My best is all I have. You're welcome to it."

He leaned closer, and Etta snatched the reports out of his view. She had the irrational urge to toss them into the hearth, but it would do little good. The words on them had already passed from the marshal's hands. And besides, if Gideon discovered that she'd destroyed kingdom property...

"By the wall," she whispered, her grip on the documents going limp. "That's why. It's why he's never trusted me. It's why he has the ring."

Nickolas stared up at her.

A helpless laugh escaped Etta's chest, ending in something of a sob. "Do you know what this means?" Not only would she have to redeem herself. Etta would have to clear her father's name as well. If he was branded a traitor, she would never receive her post.

"I do not know, as I have reminded you twice. What did you find, Antonetta?"

She marched to the writing desk. "It means you'll need to deliver another letter." And Etta would be sneaking back into her father's rooms.

THE GENERAL OF Westrende was many things, but incautious was not one of them. Traps had been set in every conceivable manner at every single access point surrounding his office. The number of guards had been increased, and only a portion of them were in uniform dress. At various positions throughout the corridor were men and women who appeared to clean, to be on their way to some other destination, or simply to be in conversation while standing conveniently in view of his rooms.

If she had been the betting sort, Etta would have placed the king's jewels that her father had told no one why he had organized the additional guards. But she was not the betting sort, and she knew her father well enough to know that the presence of so many kingsmen meant he was nowhere near his office. He would be in his rooms, and anything of real value to him would have been removed to his private vault.

She walked past a pair in cleric robes as they discussed in great detail the tapestry that hung on the opposite wall. Each glanced at her, eyes skirting her face in evidence of the fae glamour doing its work. The general's office was several corridors away from his private rooms, and with evening came the lull of activity between dinner and lights out. The halls were quiet, the few passersby seemingly uninterested in what Etta was about. It helped, no doubt, that she'd borrowed the uniform of a maid—one that she had no interest in knowing why Nickolas had on hand.

Etta's father would be in his study at that hour, the same as always. Etta would not be attempting to stroll anywhere near the place. The glamour might prevent him from recalling her features, but she could not be sure he wouldn't recognize her again, particularly if he was waiting for the return of a young female intruder. He was, surely, or he would not have loosed so many kingsmen in the corridors outside his office.

Head down, she entered the staff areas where those responsible for care of the general's wing gathered. Etta had been away for several years, but turnover was slow, and she would still know most of them by name. With a stranger's face and an Ostwind's knowledge of their own rooms, Etta would be able to get close enough, under the guise of performing staff duties, that she might slip unnoticed to the place where her father kept his most prized possessions. She might get close enough to find her way into his chambers and the vault in which he kept things he meant for no one else to see.

She fell into step with a pack of footmen, picked up a

bucket along with a group of maids, then shuffled behind a slender woman who was deftly trimming wicks and preparing rooms for the evening. Eventually, Etta was at the door to her father's sitting room, one short evasion away from the bedchamber and the vault. But as she waited for the other maid to turn away, Etta sensed movement on the opposite side of the room.

Her eyes tracked a shadow at the base of the wall near the wide fireplace, and she watched as the shape skittered into something unnatural. Etta shifted, pretending to wipe dust from a chair back as she followed its movement. It darted toward the far door, a cackle of glee erupting from the creature as it disappeared, impossibly, beneath the narrow strip between door and floor.

The maid glanced at her as if she had made the noise, but the woman's gaze skirted the glamour on Etta's face. The woman stood for a moment, as if having forgotten herself entirely, before finally returning to the task still in her hands. Etta moved closer to the door but froze when muffled voices sounded on the other side. Heart in her throat, she listened then swallowed a curse. It was her father, not in his study but in the room just beyond, a small private space that connected his suite to the one that had been her mother's.

No one should have been with him in that room, not when he'd sealed his wife's chamber from their own daughter.

Etta could not help herself, as unsafe as it was, as much as she risked. Her feet moved closer, ears pricked to pick out the second voice. It was male. Smooth. Measured in word and tone. Not at all familiar.

Etta leaned closer to the wood, her palm pressing against it while her feet remained well away from where the shadow had slipped through.

"No," her father said. "That will not do."

The other man was silent. There was a sound too light to

be certain of, and Etta's ear found the door next to her palm. *Paper*. It was the sound of rustling paper and... something else. She could not be sure what.

"I refuse." Her father again.

And the other. "Tell it, then, to the prince."

The prince. The words were a sword that cut Etta down the middle, half of her pinned to the door, the other half falling into that pit of dread and despair like so many stones her father had tossed to the bottom of a deep, dark well. She couldn't settle on a response. He could not, would not, be standing in the next room with a fae.

He was the general. An Ostwind. It was impossible.

Etta leaned back, her palm coming from the door to slide down the bare skin of her neck. The choking sensation might have been fear or anger, but she could not let it out. She could not let herself be caught. Fingers trembling, she glanced at the maid, but the woman had moved to another section of the room.

Beyond the door, Etta's father said, "And for that, you would give me your true name?"

The other voice was quiet a moment too long.

Fae, Etta's mind screamed. *It's because he's a fae.*

"A name has more value than your question implies."

The general made a dismissive sound. "Many a name would." At the noise that followed, Etta imagined her father stood. "But not yours."

Etta's racing heart froze. He could not have been fool enough to challenge a fae. But the thought was more foolish than his action. Etta's father was a general, battle trained and with an army at his back. Etta's father was the one man who might have been able to stand against all fae. Except he never had, not for her and not for her mother. He had all but vowed he never would.

"You," a voice called from inside the room, and Etta

turned, feeling the blood drain from her face as a footman in the doorway stared her down. "What are you about?"

He clearly had no idea the general was inside the next room, or a kingsman would already have been summoned for her eavesdropping. Spying on a man like the general would amount to treason.

Behind the doorway, Etta's father—the highest official of Westrende—made a deal with a Rivenwilde fae. A bigger crime, she could not imagine, aside from maybe poisoning a king. In a muffled tone, the fae spoke his side of the bargain, revealing his true name.

Etta straightened to face the footman. "A mouse."

He gave her a look.

"I thought I saw one, but.... Possibly, I only feel faint."

There was surely a more believable excuse somewhere, had Etta's mind the space to spare it, but the man only flicked a gesture that ordered her to him. He was not a small man. She supposed she could take him, but things would go much better for all involved if she could talk her way out of it. Lying was admittedly not one of her stronger skills. Shoulders dropping, she crossed the room in the least confrontational manner she could manage.

He guided her by the upper arm into the corridor. "Wait here."

Etta wondered if the face she wore looked like enough of a half-wit to lie in wait for her punishment, but she did not say so. "Of course." She clasped her fingers before her waist, head down in meek remorse. The footman strode away, likely to get a higher up and have the snooping maid who'd lingered by a restricted doorway removed from service. The book she'd come for would be permanently out of reach. Worse, her father was... had just... saints, she couldn't even think it. Her hand slid into the pocket of her gown, beneath the borrowed apron, and found her father's ring.

It was cold and hard, and so much like the truth she'd just discovered. She wanted to be sick. She wanted to turn around, stride into his rooms, and... she had no idea. But she would decide once she faced him.

Down the corridor beyond her came the echo of a quiet *snick*, and Etta glanced up in time to see a tall, dark figure exiting through one of the barred doorways to what had been her mother's rooms. The man strode away without a single look in Etta's direction, but his form flickered as his glamour revealed itself to her sight.

It was the fae who had met with her father, the fae for whom Etta had overheard a true name.

Something wild rose from her stomach to her chest, and she was moving before good sense could stop her. The maid Margaretta had no weapons—staff caught in the general's rooms with a blade would bring a far swifter response than what the footman had delivered—but Antonetta Ostwind had not been trained with sword alone. She crouched to the floor and reached inside the general's doorway to retrieve a drapery brush from the maid's supplies.

Etta's steps were silent and swift, her moves a graceful dance, her palms curved firmly around the brush as she snapped it in two.

The fae had not heard her coming and only glanced back at the sound of snapping wood.

Its jagged edge was at his neck before a lick of magic had risen to strike, Etta's words a whisper against his ear from behind him as she invoked his true name. He stilled, and she warned, "If I scent a bit of power, if you make one single flinch, so help me, I will bleed you out right here on this priceless carpet, even if your screams cost us both our lives."

Her words were a vow, and the man beneath her was as silent as a statue. Etta was not certain he had even drawn breath.

"Why were you meeting with Ostwind?" she whispered. "What business do you have with a general of Westrende?"

She felt his jaw shift in a smile. "I know who you are, Lady Ostwind. There is no need to pretend with me."

Etta pressed the stake harder against his flesh. "If you know who I am, then you know I speak the truth. Your life is worth nothing to me. Less than nothing, for it would bring me great pleasure, in fact, to rid the world of every single fae." She punctuated her last words with a deeper press of her makeshift weapon. Had it been any less dull, his blood would already have spilled. It would have been a far slower death than with a dagger, but she could not make herself care. The fae had taken everything from her, and if that was not enough, they now meddled with Westrende's general.

"Every life is worth something." His voice was calm, but Etta felt the truth in it. He believed he had something to give.

"Tell me, then. You know what I want. You know what they did to me."

"I cannot tell you that."

"Then you have nothing for me."

She braced herself, but the fae said, "Wait."

Her hand stilled, trembling, eager to be through with what would have been an especially unpleasant task.

"I cannot tell you what I am bound by edict not to speak."

But that did not mean he was bound not to speak at all. Etta had little idea what to ask of him, aside from whatever business was between Rivenwilde and her father. She didn't know what good an answer would do if she had no valid question. She would not waste the risk of a bargain if nothing useful would come of it. "Tell me what it is that you cannot speak of."

He laughed. "That would give the very game away. Do not

ask me what you have asked already. Nothing of kings and princes, nothing of generals, but anything else."

"How do I cross the wall?"

"As with any curse, speak his name, and he will come to you. The price he gives, once paid, will return what you once called yours."

She yanked him closer. "I am not fool enough to fall for that." Summoning a fae prince into Westrende was a sure way to end up regretting all she'd ever done. But the words were an echo of the painter, and while Etta may not have been able to ask a bound man what deals her father had made or what precisely the fae was about, it might gain her the power to ask it of another, someone closer to the curse that obscured her true face. "The painter."

Beneath her hold, the fae tensed.

Etta's mouth flattened into something of a grim smile. "Give me his name." The man did not respond and did not move for so long that she began to wonder if he *had* turned to stone. But he was only considering, giving thought to the bargain in the unhurried way so many fae adopted. "Time is almost up. It is this or it is nothing. His true name for your life."

A slow breath released from the form beneath her, and with it, a single word: "Elsher." As if that breath were a wind, the bargain made, the figure of the fae was gone with it, his hair sifted through her fingers like sand, his flesh no longer beneath her weapon. There was nothing but the girl who had once been Lady Ostwind, holding her broken shard of wood.

Nothing but a curse and a faceless maid who had possession of a fae's true name.

CHAPTER 16

Etta returned to the chancery wing well past dinner
to find Robert quietly reading, Tobias methodically
sorting a jar of buttons, and her roommate sleeping
facedown on a narrow bunk. Jules had left a plate of bread and
fruit beneath a thin napkin on Etta's bed. Etta sat heavily
beside the plate and unlaced her boots before carefully dropping them to the floor. She'd rinsed her hands in a basin
before returning, but the sensation of fae magic still felt too
recent. She brushed her fingertips lightly over her face. The
shape of it was the same as ever.

The bird watched her from its cage, so Etta pinched a
hunk of bread from her roll and tossed it through the bars.
The animal did not seem hale, but she wasn't about to stick
her fingers inside to find out. It pecked at the bread as any
other bird might have, and Etta went back to undressing.
Likely she was too tense for sleep, but the only way she might
sneak off alone was to be up well before dawn.

Lying back on the bed, she let the fae name repeat
through her mind. Come morning, she would say it, dagger in

hand, and Margaretta, the assistant, would have one chance to win back her true life. The lady Ostwind was ready.

HOURS BEFORE COCKCROW, Etta bolted upright in bed, her chest heaving with sharp intakes of breath. The room was dark as pitch, and no amount of blinking could erase the images of the fae from her nightmares. She grappled blindly for her clothes, not bothering to attempt donning them until she made it to the corridor. Were she to run into any guards, they would just have to accept seeing her in a shift because waiting—or waking Jules—was out of the question. The dreams had made Etta feel trapped and alone in a way she'd not felt since she was a girl pinned by fear beneath her childhood bed as the prince and his men took her mother.

With shaking hands, she tied the dress snug to her form then stepped into her boots and laced them carefully. In her left pocket was her father's ring. In her right palm, she held the dagger she'd taken from Nickolas's rooms.

He would be delivering another letter for her at dawn, one for the chancellor from Lady Ostwind herself. With any luck, Etta would have more than a single fae name. She'd have answers. Evidence. A way to get free.

She strode down the corridor, toward the most isolated and insulated storage room nearby. Not a single guard found her on the walk, but should one hear a struggle once the fae had been called, as a staff member, Etta could easily claim she'd been dragged from her rooms and that the man was trespassing on chancery property. He would be arrested. An iron-barred cell, she decided, would be as good a place as any to keep him until she had a way to prove who he was.

Edicts were not an easy thing to unwind—otherwise, she

might use the power of Elsher's true name to force him to confess. But the prince's power would supersede such a command. Etta would have to ask of the man something he would be free to give.

She lit a taper, carried it into the storage room, and placed it on a narrow ledge before she locked the door. The key went into her pocket opposite the ring, and she took one slow, deep breath as she adjusted her grip on the dagger.

Do not speak their name, her father's voice said. *Speak of them, and they will come again.*

Back against a wall of shelves, Etta whispered, "Elsher."

THE FAE FORMED like the shifting of shadow. The candle flame guttered then swelled, throwing light over the flesh of painfully familiar shapes. Dark, hollow eyes stared back at her from beneath a sharp brow. His hair was mussed—not from sleep, Etta thought, but as if he never bothered grooming it into a style. The same scents of orange oil and musk rose from him, along with smoke and roasting meat.

His mouth slid into a hard line, his gaze never leaving hers. "Lady Ostwind. How good of you to ruin my night."

She held the blade forward. "I call you to bargain. A true answer in exchange for your life."

He scoffed. "My life belongs to another. Good luck winning it back."

She tipped her chin toward the door. "Your freedom, then, for without that trade, you cannot escape."

He crossed his arms and scowled. "What business have you with me? I no longer possess your trade. I'm bound in more ways than either of us could count. There is no threat you might offer me that others have not already."

Etta flicked the dagger tip to his chest above his crossed arms. A gold button *tinked* against a jar on the shelf beside them, and the fae gasped in outrage when he realized she'd cut it from his coat. She raised a brow. "What is happening between the prince and my father?"

"I cannot answer that. I am bound."

"Why has he come for me? Because of my mother? Because we can see?"

His arms dropped to his sides. "You think so highly of yourself. A great Ostwind, as lofty as your father."

Another button clinked off the shelf then clattered to the floor.

He huffed. "Call his name if you want your answers. I have nothing for you."

"We both know I cannot do that." Not until she had the upper hand—any hand, even a stake in the game. The dagger shifted in her grip. "Why you? Why not him? Why not face me himself?"

He turned up a palm. "I have a talent for glamour."

"And the prince knows I can see. Was he testing you or testing me?"

Elsher chuckled.

Etta moved closer.

He held up a hand. "You're wasting time for the both of us, Antonetta. Might as well get some sleep." He leaned in. "The sands are spending. Best to enjoy what days you have left."

A weight settled in the pit of Etta's stomach. "What do you mean?"

His mouth twisted into a cruel smile. "Did you think the curse had no limit? That you might live forever in this state of in-between?"

"There's a clock? You told me nothing of the sort."

He shrugged, sliding a hand over his chest where the row

of buttons once was. His brows drew together as he picked at a loose thread. "Why should I? I left it right there for you to see."

She stuck the tip of the blade to his chest, not gently.

He glanced up at her.

"Tell me," she ordered, "in plain words."

"The painting, of course." He reached into his pocket and drew out a bright-red apple. He tossed it into the air, but Etta did not catch it. It smashed onto the floor, cracking open to splatter bits of pulp up his trouser leg and Etta's skirt. He frowned. "That was all the fruit I had with me. There's no call for—"

His words cut off as her dagger slid from his chest to the soft bit of flesh beneath his chin. "You're still here."

"Yes," he managed despite the clearly uncomfortable angle of his head with a knife at its base. "That one was free."

"Because you were meant to tell me days ago, when you first set the curse."

He did not respond. Etta swore.

"There is nothing more you can ask me tonight," he told her. "Why not just let me go?"

Etta's dagger inched higher. "You have given me nothing." It meant she could call on him again, whenever she wanted. But if she did, the next time, he would be ready. "What does the prince want with Westrende?"

A sound like a laugh moved his chest. "That is no secret, either."

"And yet, somehow, no one here seems aware." She jerked the blade away from his jaw.

His depthless eyes met hers.

"What does he want with Westrende?" she asked again. "Why us?" Her mother, her father, and Etta herself... it could not have been a coincidence. "Why does he send his men here to meddle and curse while he sits so easily on his throne? What is his goal?"

Elsher's teeth flashed in something that was not a smile. "Why, to unrend the kingdoms, of course."

Etta's insides went cold. She unlocked the door and set the fae free. With the bargain unmade, he would be forced to walk back through the castle grounds, into the forest, beyond the filigree wall, and past the Rive, the ancient boundary that had split the kingdoms in two.

Unrend, Elsher had said.

Fates protect us all.

She strode through the chancery corridors, fuming that the fae had done her so wrong. She'd not been warned of a clock on her curse and had no idea where the painting might be.

"Why, I left it with you," he'd said when she'd asked. "As part of the curse, it will never stray far."

All along, it had been right there, beneath the guard of the chancery. It had found its way there as evidence, no doubt, in the case against whoever would be blamed for the death of Lord Barrett.

The corridors were still dim as she slipped between one office and the next, on watch for patrolling kingsmen. Dawn light had not yet begun to peek through the widows when she finally came into the records room where Tobias spent so many of his hours, toiling away. Stepping past racks and shelves, Etta held her candle high.

A canvas-covered easel stood among stacks of crates and boxes. She crept forward, hating the fear that crawled over her skin. She knew what was beneath the drape of fabric, even before she reached to pull it down. But once she did, the fear grew worse. The portrait that stared back at her, though it was hers, was not the same as it had been the week before.

Narrowed eyes glared out from a face that had lost all hint

of the hopeful expression Elsher had painted into it. Instead, the visage spoke of vengeance. It held a horrid sense of loss, anger, and a fruitless desire to undo what could not be changed. The hidden fox now showed its teeth, its shadow long in spiky strips of black. The ship in her hair had sails that appeared weathered, and the goose was missing patches of feathers. The ribbons laced through Etta's mouth remained, as if tying her from speaking—of what, she didn't know. From revealing fae secrets, perhaps, or from convincing a soul of who she truly was.

Etta moved nearer, standing so close that she might have reached out to brush her fingertips over the paint. But she did not touch it, not when she could not pull her eyes away from the apple in the figure's hands.

Young and hale, the painted fingers cradled their prize in the way they'd done before, but instead of the bright, shining shape it had been when Etta had first seen it, the apple was dark, withered and rotting, its skin and flesh decaying even as she watched. The paint was crazed over its surface, fine cracks spreading from it like shattered glass.

It was her clock. And time was running out. When the apple was gone, so would be Etta, snatched across the Rive as a prisoner to the fae and their magic, never to see the light of day again. No one would ever know what had become of her.

A sound echoed from the main office, and she glanced up, surprised to find that dawn light was rising in a gray haze through the windows. Having no idea how long she'd stood mesmerized, she blew out the flame of her candle then set the holder on the floor at her feet. A tendril of smoke rose between her glamoured face and the more familiar one on the canvas.

Easing a hand around the grip of her dagger, she stepped closer still. The portrait seemed to pulse with magic, with the strange sense of falling, as if she stared into the depths of a well and she might tumble weightlessly in at any moment.

She knew what waited on the other side.

Etta drove the blade into the canvas, her loathing for the fae and their curse pushing her to destroy everything they had ever done. She would shred it to ribbons and burn the remains. The dagger cut effortlessly through the paint and cloth, but the magic was not destroyed. Heat worse than any pain she had ever felt seared through her arm. She stumbled backward, knocking into a crate before her back hit a sturdy shelf.

Palm wrapped about her forearm and eyes on the painted girl in the marshal's coat, Etta slid helplessly down the shelf to sit on the floor. Her feet splayed out before her as she stared at the portrait, Nickolas's dagger on the floor beneath it, and morning light shining through the slice of canvas in the center of the figure's arm, just where Etta's own arm was flayed and bleeding.

A gasp sounded from the doorway. Tobias, stock-still, watched in horror. Jules was suddenly beside him, her hand on his shoulder and her quiet assurances in his ear as she pressed him aside.

Once the boy was gone, Jules rushed to kneel at Etta's side.

"Let me," she murmured, prying Etta's fingers away from the weeping wound. Jules winced, made a sound of dismay, then followed Etta's gaze to the portrait of Lady Antonetta Ostwind. An unusual expression—too quick to make out—crossed Jules's face. In a blink, her attention was back on the wound. She tied a handkerchief tightly around it and urged Etta to her feet. "Come now. We need to get this washed and stitched. Hurry," she added, and Etta tore her gaze from the portrait to truly take in Jules. "Before anyone else comes and tries to make a fuss," she said, as if the justification made any sense at all. Someone would absolutely make a fuss. Lady Ostwind's portrait had just been stabbed, and Etta was bleeding all over herself.

"There goes another dress," Etta said numbly as she stared down at the mess.

"Come," Jules said again.

Etta did go, if for no other reason than she couldn't stomach one more moment in the presence of the portrait. But before they left the room, Jules crossed to the easel and tossed the drape over the canvas once more. Without a single look at Etta, she kicked the dagger beneath a shelf. When she returned to Etta's side, Jules spoke not a word of what she had done but only led Etta from the room.

SETTLED on a low bench in a quiet storeroom, Etta stared at the narrow gash that crossed her arm. It still felt strangely hot, not unlike the stinging cuts and scrapes the lesser fae had given her as a girl and, more recently, in the forest outside the kingdom borders. Jules wrung a cloth out over a basin before pressing it to the wound with a click of her tongue.

"You aren't going to ask what happened?"

Etta's tone had been cagey, but Jules's reply was subdued. "We all have our moments. If you had wanted to tell me, then you would have."

Etta watched the gentle pressure and graceful movements of Jules's practiced hands. There was something too delicate and deliberate about it, something very unlike the girl who fumbled scrolls and napped like a drunken sailor. "Where did you learn to care for wounds?"

The pressure from Jules's ministrations stilled, but only for an instant. One of her shoulders shifted in a shrug. "I had a half dozen brothers growing up. One was always in a tumble of one sort or another."

"Where are they now?"

Jules's gaze met hers. "Would you like to discuss our pasts, my lady?"

"No," Etta answered truthfully.

"Something else, then?"

"Do you mean the lady Ostwind?" Etta asked.

Jules's eyes went back to her work. "If you wish."

"Yes," Etta said after a moment. "I would like to talk about Lady Ostwind."

Jules tugged the needle through Etta's arm and tied off the first suture.

Etta released her gritted teeth to ask, "Why does the chancellor hate them?"

The needle missed its mark. "Them?"

"The general and his daughter. He's pitted himself against the family, has he not?"

"My lady," Jules started, but Etta cut her off.

"The truth would be helpful."

A strange quirk tilted the edge of Jules's lip before her mouth went into a thin line. "And yet you're the one who drove a dagger though a portrait of an Ostwind."

"It's hideous."

Jules made no reply.

Etta shoved a loose lock of hair behind her ear with the arm that wasn't being prodded. "The chancellor believes her a criminal. Unfit for office."

Jules worked in silence for a long moment. When she finally spoke, her tone was careful. "Gideon wasn't raised in the way a person might expect."

She cut another suture, one more in a very neat row of small, close ties over a dark line that made Etta's stomach turn. Etta had seen blood often enough, but it was somehow worse when a wound was formed by magic. Worse still was to know that anyone might cut her in two just by slicing up a cursed bit of canvas.

Jules said, "He had to work very hard to get where he is."

Etta bristled. "Every Westrende official works hard. They give up everything just for the chance."

The needle stabbed a little fiercer into Etta's arm. "Some start with much less and lose much more."

"His uncle is steward. His mother captained a ship. He'd have been raised in luxury, with the best training." She frowned. "It's not as if a man like that has ever missed a meal."

Jules gave her a look. "You truly don't know?"

"Know what?"

Jules wiped a towel over the skin surrounding the wound then shifted the bowl of supplies out of the way to settle beside Etta. "Lord Alexander was raised by his mother's cousin. His parents were gone before he'd turned one and ten. He may have possessed the title of lord, but a sailing mother and a military father did not make for a stable home life. Once they were gone, their estate was seized by an uncle on his father's side. Apparently, Gideon's parents made no arrangements to protect their sole heir. I take it there were a few years where he struggled in ways difficult to imagine." She gave Etta a pointed look. "Ways that he refuses to discuss. The relative who finally took him in was a clerk of sorts, an assistant to the magistrate. He was in need of a strong set of arms, most likely. He was a... difficult man, by all accounts. But with time, he became something of a mentor to a young boy who had no one else. When one has very little, any scrap of security can feel a great deal more valuable than it appears on paper."

Etta had known nothing of the sort. Only sparse bits of

information had reached her at school, and Nickolas had clearly left out the most pertinent facts.

Jules folded the cloth into a neat square. "Two years back, that man was killed."

Killed. Not died. Murdered. Etta's voice was barely above a whisper. "How?"

"He happened across information that cost him his life." At Etta's intense look, Jules shrugged. "Something he reported to the magistrate. An investigation followed. The evidence disappeared before charges could be brought. It was all very hushed." She stood.

"Wait—"

Jules bent to pick up the bowl of supplies and tossed a gauzy wrap to Etta. "That's all I know. But had you given the man a chance, you would have found that our chancellor has reason to operate on such a hard line."

"I don't—it's not about giving him a chance." It was impossible to defend her situation, not when she was meant to be Margaretta, family friend of Nickolas Brigham, who had no higher connection to the Ostwinds or the law. "I only wanted to understand and to see that the lady was treated fairly, given her own chance."

At the door, Jules gave Etta a fleeting glance over her shoulder. "My lady, you will not find a man more honorable than Gideon Alexander."

CHAPTER 17

Etta awoke with a splitting headache and a stinging throb in her arm. After washing up the night before, she'd fallen into bed, but no amount of sleep could undo what she had done. Jules served her black tea and fresh biscuits, but her sympathy did not extend far enough to release Etta from the day's work.

She had so much to do, not the least of which was to find a way across the wall without calling a deadly prince. Whatever business the fae had with her father, whatever was behind the misfortunes of the prospects for king, those tasks would have to wait. Etta's time was running out. She had to break the curse.

"More sorting and filing today," Jules said over an armful of scrolls, "in the chancellor's office."

"Right." Etta rose to her feet without a single swear at the fates that had her tied to a job when she had more important things to do. She needed to find a way free of the chancery's watch, and it could not wait until her next day off the following week.

She tugged her dress back into place, making certain the

gauze covering her wound was well hidden. As her mind rummaged through potential plans to retrieve her father's book and possible questions she might trade the fae whose true name she held, Etta strode through the main office with her head held high.

Her feet stumbled to a halt when a shadow crossed her path.

Etta gaped, and her hand moved automatically to her waist. But she wore no blade. Around her, time carried on, as if not a soul was aware of the danger they were in.

Hurrying past with a stack of boxes, Robert bumped into Etta's shoulder then stopped to apologize. "I didn't see you." His gaze followed hers. "Oh, my lady, this is the clerk, Eldon. Have you not been introduced?"

A pair of dark, hollow eyes rose to hers. *Fae*, Etta's mind screamed even as the man offered her a wicked grin.

"No, Robert, the lady and I have not been formally introduced. Though I've heard much of her."

Etta's mouth snapped closed. She managed a single, sharp nod. The fae's gaze remained on hers, the face beneath his glamour as plain as pikestaff in the well-lit room. His true form was wild and beastly, despite the drab robe and neat haircut the others would see.

"My lord," Tobias said from across the room, "the delivery you asked about has just come in."

The fae's attention shifted to the boy. "Ah, yes. Thank you. I'll be on my way." He inclined his head to Etta. "My lady."

Her feet were moving before he had a chance even to gather his things. She would not stand in the middle of the office when it was clear he meant to move past her. She shot into the chancellor's office and slammed the door behind her.

Gideon glanced up from the rack of bound documents he'd been searching. She crossed the distance in a few long strides, grabbed hold of his sleeve, then yanked him with her around a tall shelf. She glanced at the closed door then shoved him another step back to peer around the corner, watching.

"Margaretta." Gideon's tone was firm, chiding, and more than a bit confounded.

Etta spun, covering his mouth with a palm and making a hushing sound before she could think better of it. His eyes went wide, and she snatched her hand back. They stood in silence for a moment, Etta's heart racing and Gideon by all appearances baffled. She grabbed hold of him again, this time by the wrist, and drew him through the door to the room where they'd sparred.

The latch no more than clicked behind them before the massive head of a sleeping Clara snapped up in attention. She was on her feet, coming at them so fast all Etta had time to do was turn and grimace. The dog slammed into Etta's back, shoving her into Gideon's front and knocking them both against the closed door in her excitement. Gideon's hands were on Etta's waist as if by instinct, steadying her before his fingers shifted into a softer grip. Etta was still, her entire body pressed to his. Her cheek brushed his neck as the dog danced against the pair enthusiastically, Etta's pulse still racing hard from her encounter with the fae, and Gideon surely having no conceivable idea what she was about. His throat moved in a swallow. His fingers flexed. Etta dared not look at him.

"Clara," he finally commanded. "Down."

The dog did not sit down. Instead, at the sound of her name she wriggled closer, rapturously licking toward Gideon's cheek with her paws heavy against Etta's back. She held her arms rigid. Fighting a creature was all well and good, but she could not deal with... *this.*

Letting go of Etta's waist, Gideon reached past her to shove the dog away. Etta pressed her face into the crook of his neck to avoid a hot, wet dog muzzle from becoming intimate with her nose and mouth. When the beast snuffled her ear, she made a sound of distressed revulsion, and Gideon spun the pair of them so that Etta's back was to the door and he could settle Clara down.

Etta watched, shaking her arms in an attempt at composing herself as Gideon led the dog to the next room and shut the beast inside. He stood at the closed door, his palm on the wood for a very long moment before he turned suddenly back to Etta, apparently having recalled that something had gone wildly wrong.

"The clerk," Etta explained. "Eldon. How long has he been on staff?"

Gideon's brow drew together. "What has that to do with—"

"How long?" Etta stepped forward then froze before moving back once more to press herself to the door. She couldn't decide which might be worse, if the fae man were to come through after them or if he stood outside, listening. There was no way to know where he was.

She rushed toward Gideon, pulling him by the arm as she moved to cross the room. He was apparently becoming accustomed to being handled, because he followed without dispute as Etta led him to a cabinet and wedged them both into the narrow space behind it.

"What has he been doing, this Eldon? What work has he shown interest in? And who did he replace?" By the wall, first, the fae disguised as her painter, then the one meeting with the general, and now, a third posing as clerk. It was as if they'd infiltrated the entire kingdom while she'd been away. The memory of Lord Barrett's body in a dark pool on the polished floor made her stomach turn. It was impossible to say how many other men they'd done away with to take their place.

Gideon's expression made clear he had no idea what she was on about. Then, softly, he asked, "My lady, has the lord done something to you, acted in a way that has made you feel unsafe?"

Unsafe was precisely how Etta felt. The fae had taken residence inside the castle and maneuvered themselves near positions of real power. She didn't know if she would ever feel safe again. "Yes," she said. "But not how you think."

Etta couldn't let Gideon accuse him of anything that she might actually have to prove. No one could see through fae glamour but her, and unless the clerk had left a trail of whatever bad things he was up to, an investigation would only reveal that Margaretta was not a real person, that she and Nickolas had forged documents and inserted Etta into the very office of the man she had accused. Her head hurt. Her wound throbbed. The magic on her skin tingled hotly, sharply. Fae brazen enough to lay a curse on a general's daughter was beginning to seem the least of Westrende's problems.

Gideon's expression had gone deadly serious. He made to reach for her then apparently thought better of it. He stepped closer, despite that she was near enough to hear his heartbeat—though that might have been her own. Saints, it was too warm behind the shelf. Maybe she could crawl out of a window.

Gideon's voice was low. "I understand that you might be hesitant to say. But whatever he has done, my lady, it will be handled discreetly."

Etta ran a palm over her face. "Do not remove him. Do not tell him I've spoken a single word against him, please. I'll handle it. I just need..." Time. She needed time, and she needed the cursed fae to give her a break.

Gideon gave a swift nod. "Whatever you need, it is yours. But until then, you're to stay at my side."

"What? No."

"I insist, my lady. If he is a danger to you—"

"What about Jules and the others? Will you have the entire chancery constantly at your side as well?"

"Jules is protected."

Etta's protest drew up short.

Gideon apparently had no intention of explaining the remark. He took hold of her elbow. "I've a meeting, in fact, if you'll—" His words cut off at her wince, and he glanced down, finding the edge of gauze that peeked from beneath her sleeve.

She tried to jerk her arm away, but Gideon held fast. He slid the fabric up to reveal the bandage. His gaze met hers.

"It wasn't him. Saints, I only cut myself, that's all. It's nothing."

"Etta." His voice held the edge of something painful. "This is not a minor wound." His fingers hovered over the bandage, the fabric wrapped as wide as his palm. She had the sense he wanted to tear it away and see what hid beneath. He looked at her. "If you're in trouble, you need to tell me so I know how to help." His gaze was intent.

Etta tugged her arm from his grasp. "You can help me by saying nothing of the clerk and by letting me go about my work as if this never happened."

"I can do the first. The second is not negotiable." He glanced at the light through the windows. "I'll be late for my meeting. Come along, and bring something to take notes. It needs to appear that you are needed."

Etta pressed her fingers to the bridge of her nose, refusing to consider what her life had become. "Where are we going?"

He straightened, adjusting the lay of his chancellor's coat. "To the council chambers. I've a private meeting with General Ostwind."

"General Ost—" Etta's words cut off as she realized she was speaking to Gideon's back.

He refused to hear her objections, walking away from her as if she were a dog meant to follow.

She did follow.

"I've received another letter from Lady Ostwind," he said.

When he turned to look at her, Etta had to force the expression from her face. She'd forgotten about the follow-up letter she'd sent with Nickolas.

Gideon's voice dropped. "You might as well know, now that you'll be privy to the general's complaint."

"His complaint?" Etta whispered.

Gideon picked up a bound book from his desk. "He hasn't taken well to the knowledge that his daughter has been in contact with a mere chancellor more than she has him." He handed her a book of blank pages for her to note whatever of import was said.

"Of course she's written you," Etta said. "She has a task to complete."

He turned to stride toward the office door, and at his gesture, Etta followed. She took a hasty extra step to catch up to him.

"Lady Ostwind is very driven, is she not?"

As he passed through the doorway, Gideon gave her a sidelong glance. "I suppose that's one way of putting it."

"How else?" Etta asked. "How would you put it?"

Gideon did not answer, his attention on the room. Searching for the clerk, no doubt. The man had no earthly idea that he'd been working with a fae all along.

"He's gone out," Etta said coldly. "Something about a delivery."

Gideon minutely adjusted his stride, but only a fool could have missed that he was suddenly walking shoulder to shoulder with her like a kingsman on guard. He gave a small nod to Jules, whose surprised gaze tracked them crossing the room, but Gideon made no explanations. He didn't have to. He was the chancellor.

They stepped through the wide entrance doors into a busy corridor, and something dipped in Etta's gut. She had to get out of this. There was no way she could sit in a room with her father and—fae glamour or no—he not realize that she was the girl he'd seen in his office.

She considered faking an illness, but one look at Gideon's dark eyes subtly searching every face in the corridor made clear he would not let it go. She didn't know what she'd been thinking. She never should have asked him about the clerk, not when Jules or Robert or any of the others would have given her whatever they knew without risk of—whatever this fresh abyss was.

Training had given her the tools she needed. She'd been in Gideon's presence for more than a week. She knew what would make him respond. There was nothing she could offer to stop him outside of something more urgent than his meeting with the general. Something that would be important enough to tempt him to break his word.

Something that would allow her to kill two birds with one stone.

"I can give you information about General Ostwind."

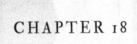

CHAPTER 18

Gideon stopped in his tracks.

"It's something of great import to the kingdom" —she hesitated and lowered her voice—"with regard to the wall."

He took hold of her elbow and ushered her into a lesser-used corridor, waiting until no one was in sight before speaking again. "What are you saying?" They were face to face, his hushed whisper barely echoing off the walls.

"I can show you. I can give you evidence, but it has to be now—while the general is occupied with council business."

Gideon stared at her, the cogs clearly turning in his mind. "You're asking me to—" He shook himself, apparently unable to even think it. "This goes against my every duty, the very order of precedence."

Etta leaned closer. "The marshal hasn't managed it. You know that. He's had years to uncover secrets. What's he done? Filled your office with useless reports?"

Gideon's eyes narrowed. "I knew not to trust Nickolas Brigham."

"Enough already with Nickolas. He didn't show me the reports. What is your problem with the man, anyway?

"He's a rake and a gossip and apparently trades information for..." His angry hiss cut off at Etta's expression.

She inched closer still. "You think I would be so easily fooled? That I would fall apart over a few pretty words and a man who did nothing more than give me his gaze?"

Gideon was petulant. "I've seen it happen."

Etta crossed her arms, furious that he was still on about the scene he'd caught in the hall. "Truly? You'll judge him so harshly when you yourself were pressed up against me not a quarter hour ago?"

His face went pale, guilt washing every feature. He didn't know she was Lady Ostwind. He thought she was a member of his staff.

"My lady, I—" He made as if to reach for her then snatched back his hands. "You have my sincerest apologies. I never meant to—if I have made you feel uncomfortable..." He frowned. "Of course I have. I've put you in the worst sort of position, and I'm sorry. I vow that I'll never again—"

Etta held up a hand. "Please. It's been clear since the moment we met that you're not the sort to become impassioned enough to cavort in a public corridor. I doubt you've ever been infatuated in your life."

He stared at her dumbly.

Glancing at the connecting corridor to be certain no one might overhear, she said, "I can show you." Her gaze came back to his just as color rose in his neck. "The general," she snapped. "I can show you what I meant about the general."

Gideon took a step back. "My lady, I think we need a moment to... No, I'm already late to the meeting. Let's go. We can discuss this later." Giving her a look, he added, "Maybe." He shook his head, as if to dispel the thoughts that must have been racing through it.

Etta reclaimed the distance he'd made. Facing her father would be a disaster. She would be arrested and thrown into a cell, offered no chance to break the curse before time ran out. She needed to give Gideon something he wanted. "Trust me with this," she vowed, "and I will tell you about the clerk and what happened to my arm."

She had him. She could see it in his eyes. As chancellor, he had to discover if his clerk was a danger, and Etta knew he bore a great distrust of the Ostwinds. Two birds, one stone.

"No," Gideon said as they stood outside the general's private suite. "Absolutely not."

"Would you keep it down?" she hissed. "If we get caught before we have the evidence in hand, not even a chancellor will be able to talk his way out of it."

"Do you understand how many laws you're about to break? Have you no shred of decency or, saints protect us, self-preservation?"

Etta blew out a long breath. "I do not have time to debate this. If you care about the kingdom at all, if you have any loyalty to your post and to your mentor, you'll do this. You'll see what I have to show you, and you'll understand things you wish you'd never known."

"My mentor." His tone was level.

"Jules told me. I can see now why you don't trust the general. He does look guilty, after all, does he not?" When he didn't reply, Etta glanced back at him. She was being a bit crude, but there wasn't a moment to spare. "You believe he's behind all of it—that he wants to keep his position as head of council and that someone you cared about was killed for getting too close to the truth." Etta swallowed hard, praying that whatever evidence the chancellor had already gathered was false, that it had been put in place by the fae to make him look guilty. But if her father truly was involved, she could not save him. No one could, not if he'd bargained with a fae prince for the security of Westrende. "You think that General Ostwind is responsible for what's been happening to the prospects for king. We are paces away from the truth. If you follow me inside, I'll give you what you need. You have only to trust me." She placed her hand on the lever to her father's room. "And if not, then I suppose you'll just have to ask our current marshal to throw me in a cell to rot."

Before he had time to respond, Etta opened the door and stepped through. A relieved breath slipped from her as she saw the lavish room was empty. Had there been a kingsman on guard or even a maid present, she'd no idea what might have happened.

As it was, Gideon was trying desperately to snatch at her gown and drag her back. "Etta," he demanded.

It only made her feet move faster. She had needed him in order to get closer to the general's rooms unsuspected, but he was only a liability moving forward.

A low oath escaped him as they entered the general's bedroom, Gideon's entire posture making clear that he could not believe he'd allowed himself to come so far. But Etta worked quickly, rolling the edge of carpet up beneath the bed.

"Help me with this," she said, shouldering the weight of it to slide the secret floor panel aside. It wouldn't budge, so she raised up to rummage through the items in her father's nightstand while Gideon knelt at her side.

"You have to stop," he said.

Etta found a comb and tried to pry up the board. It wasn't thin enough. She turned to Gideon and yanked one of the metal bands from his coat. As he reached for it, clearly hesitant to grab her bodily after the conversation they'd just had, she shoved the metal between one plank and the next and levered the wood up with the weight of a forearm. Before Gideon had changed his mind about taking hold of her, Etta had opened the vault and was reaching inside among her father's things: a master key, private letters, and an ancient leather-bound book.

Gideon made a sound and shifted backward, but Etta could not focus on him. Flipping through the pages, she nearly crowed when she found the passage she was looking for. No time to celebrate one small victory when her battle had just begun. She turned to face Gideon, both of them kneeling on the floor beside her father's bed. She would have to be fast, but the look on his face said she'd shocked him enough with the fae-marked book to gain a moment's head start.

"Trust me," she said. "You do not want him to know how you've found this. Speak nothing of me, of Margaretta, or you'll look as guilty as the rest of us in the eyes of the law."

His mouth opened in question, but in one fluid motion, Etta stood and tore out three pages before tossing the book to the floor at Gideon's knees.

She was running before she'd taken another breath. The bedroom door slammed behind her, and she turned the key, but she wasn't free—inside the sitting room was a footman, his shocked gaze swinging to hers at the sound of the door. She didn't waste time by confronting him but took the shorter route to her mother's rooms instead of the exit. The footman gave chase then rammed into the door as Etta shut it behind her. Her father's key was already in the lock, and she was on her way to the next room. She had seconds before the call went up. Kingsmen were everywhere inside the castle and on the grounds, and one alarm would be all it took before she would have nowhere to turn.

She burst into her mother's bedroom, the sight of it after so many years knocking the breath from her, but Etta could not stop. She had no time for memories, only action. Only to flee.

The last door hadn't been opened in ages, and she had to

shoulder into it hard. Tumbling into the corridor, she glanced frantically toward the entrance to her father's suite farther down.

It was not a kingsman who stared back at her but Gideon, eyes dark, knuckles white with their grip on her father's book. He moved, and Etta ran as fast as her feet would carry her. She reached to hike up the length of her skirts then vaulted over a railing and into a memorial gallery scattered with giant pale sculptures of dead heroes of Westrende.

"Margaretta," Gideon called from behind her, "stop, or I will sound the alarm."

His voice was too close, his footsteps coming too fast. He was going to catch her. If he did, she would never get free. Ducking beneath the carved hooves of a rearing horse, Etta glanced back. Gideon was only paces away. Beyond him, past the gallery rail, strode a line of kingsmen—the general's personal guard.

Etta cursed, spun around a statue of a man holding a sapling and a massive sword, and darted toward the courtyard. Bright light shone on delicate topiaries, and dappled shadows scattered the path. She leapt over a bench, through a trellis of roses... and ran face-first into the chancellor of Westrende.

His arms slammed around her, caging her, and momentum nearly knocked them both to the ground. Too many footsteps sounded on the paths beyond the greenery, their cadence that of soldiers on the run. She was done. It was over.

Etta stared up into Gideon's eyes.

"Margaretta," he said softly.

In reply, Etta whispered the only word she could find. *"Elsher."*

CHAPTER 19

The fae shimmered into existence through the shifting shadows of a willow tree, his fingers midway through fastening the buttons of a fine silk coat. He glanced up at Etta and cursed. "Must you," he said drearily, "always?"

Gideon was so startled that his grip eased, but only for a moment. He pushed Etta behind him. She did not know what he saw, because the fae in question had been masquerading as the now dead Lord Barrett.

She didn't bother to ask, shoving past Gideon to address the fae. "Help me escape."

Elsher glanced at the flashes of red and black though the trees, uniforms of the soldiers who would soon be upon them. "No."

Etta stepped closer. "Get me to the forest, and I'll relinquish your name." At his narrow look, she added, "If you do not, I vow to call on you every hour of every day. You'll have no more time than to return home before my words will drag you back again."

Beyond the trees, one of the kingsmen barked a command.

"And I'll likely be calling you to a damp, dreary prison cell," Etta said.

"You are a menace," he growled.

"Then end it. Help me."

His gaze roamed the courtyard then briefly shifted to Gideon in his fine uniform coat for a once-over. Etta opened her mouth to refine her terms, to shout, "only me," but Elsher tossed up a hand.

"Done," he said with a self-satisfied smile.

Etta's protests went unheeded, and a heartbeat later, when she was rolling across a bed of moss, the fae man's chuckle vibrated through her despite that he was nowhere to be found. She cursed, coming to a stop flat on her back, limbs splayed. It wasn't a heartbeat more before Gideon tumbled after—thrown a little harder, it seemed, though Etta's body worked well enough as a stop.

She grunted when his form collided with hers, knocking a huff of breath from his chest on impact. He lay atop her for a moment, evidently stunned, before his face rose from its nest among the material of her bodice. His eyes met hers. He blinked.

When his senses returned, he scrambled backward, but Etta only groaned.

He froze, midway to his feet, to stare at her. "Are you hurt?"

She pushed up on her elbows to look at him then purpose-fully shifted her gaze to the surrounding forest. Gideon, apparently still stunned, took a moment to follow her indica-tion. He stood slowly but did not entirely straighten, perched among the ferns as if in a ready crouch.

"There it is," she muttered at his realization of their surroundings. She shoved up to stand. He would be a minute, processing the idea, she assumed, so she glanced down at herself to check what might be amiss. The gown had come through their tumble well enough, but one foot was bare and sinking into the blanket of soft earth and moss. Searching the ground they'd crossed, Etta moved to fetch her missing slipper. When she picked it up to shake out the hunks of greenery, she glanced again at Gideon. "What did you do about the general's footman, anyway?"

He made no sign of hearing. Etta pulled the folded pages from the pocket of her skirt. Her father's guards had either seen their chancellor running after a faceless girl who'd escaped the general's rooms and had assembled in record time, or they'd been lying in wait for another attempt. She wondered what the general thought of his intruder and whether he had any idea that what Etta had said before was true—she was his daughter—or if he suspected she was just part of another fae ruse, aiming to manipulate whatever bargain he had made. It was very possible she'd avoided both time in a cell and torture. To the last, he would refuse to acknowledge that it might be her.

She supposed the truth would be harder to discern without the gift of sight, but it didn't make forgiving him for what he'd done any easier.

"What... just... happened?"

"Ah," Etta said, not glancing up from the papers. "You're back." She held a hand in the direction of the castle. "You'll need to walk that direction and quickly, and do not stop to touch any animals or trees. Keep your face up, eyes on the sun, and should you find yourself turned around, start again. Do not shout for help until you're clear of the trees. It's important."

Etta felt his stare.

"I'm sorry," she said. "You don't... well, I won't say you

don't deserve this, but you have my sympathy nonetheless. Just go, and do it quickly."

"Are we in the greenwood?" Gideon's voice was a croak.

He turned slowly, and Etta could not help but glance up at him.

His tone rose, words slow and wavering. "Is that *the wall*?"

Etta waited until he looked back at her. "Yes."

He rushed to close the distance. "I do not understand what happened, but we need to go. Now."

She sighed. "That's exactly what I was trying to tell you. Go." She gestured in a shooing motion, but Gideon did not move.

"My lady—"

"We have little time, either of us, and you're not going to like anything I'm about to do. Please, my lord, run from these woods and do not look back."

"I can't leave you here."

Her eyes pressed closed for a long moment. She truly wished she had her sword. "Oh," she said, reaching forward to draw Gideon's from the sheath at his side. "This will work."

He stared at her.

She held firm on the sword in case he decided to attempt taking it back. "I'm protected now, and you've some sort of dagger or something on you, I'm sure. Best we part ways and you return to the castle before General Ostwind thinks you're in on the... whatever this is."

He was silent for a long moment. "Have you lost your mind?"

"My face, in fact. Please go."

His expression hardened. "Margaretta, I do not know what is happening, but I refuse to leave you alone *at the wall*."

She strode past him. "I assure you, you do not want to stay at my side."

Standing square with the wall, not near enough to sense

its magic, Etta drew out the notebook Gideon had given her. She etched a decent copy of the image beneath the glamour the wall projected—the section where she would make her attempt—then scratched out a hasty note for her father so that he would know what had become of her, should the worst happen. She ripped the page free of its binding, folded it deftly, then passed it to Gideon, who'd moved beside her.

"For General Ostwind."

Gideon had been watching her work, his gaze moving slowly from Etta's profile to the words, and his eyes met hers. Recognition fought with the confusion in his expression. She had forgotten the hours Gideon had spent studying the handwriting of Lady Ostwind.

"It was you," he said. "You forged those letters so that you could—what? Deceive me into handing over the investigations and reports? Are you some sort of foreign agent? Or are you working for someone inside of Westrende?"

"I realize this is a waste of breath, but here it is. Those letters were not a forgery. The face I'm wearing is. It's a curse set upon me by the prince of the fae—" A little rumble of magic swelled beneath Etta's feet, and she swallowed hard, lowering her voice. "You've been deceived, as has the rest of the kingdom. The fae walk among us, and they're closer every day to committing an unspeakable crime." She would not bring the word "unrend" to life, not so near the wall. "If no one else will protect us, then it falls to me."

"Margaretta," he started, but her look cut him off.

"I am not and have never been Margaretta. There is no Margaretta. I'm Antonetta. An Ostwind, the very one you claimed unfit for the position of marshal. My handwriting looks like Lady Ostwind's because I'm her. And not you, not my father, not one fool person in the entire kingdom will hear me out or come to my aid." She jabbed a finger toward the wall. "I am Lady Antonetta Ostwind, and I'm going to go through that wall to steal back my face. I'm going to end whatever foolishness is keeping the council from recognizing the truth. I'm going to do whatever I can to save myself and this kingdom." She leaned nearer, her grip tightening on the sword. "I dare you to try to stop me."

THE SPEECH HAD DONE LITTLE good to convince Gideon of anything, but Etta felt better for having said it. She turned to face the monstrosity of twisted metal masquerading as a beautiful stone work of art. Behind her, Gideon muttered something, but she had decided to steadfastly ignore him so that he might go away. The moment he was out of sight, she would perform the magic to open the wall.

"An-ton-etta," a low voice spoke in a menacing sort of singsong, and Etta knew right away that something had gone horribly wrong.

Sword raised, she spun to find, standing casually among the brush and briars as if it were the topiary gardens Etta had just left, *him*. The prince of the fae, as real and solid as any man. He gave her a wicked, terrifying grin.

She stepped back, her heart in her throat. "I did not call you."

The words were only a breath, barely more than a whisper, but the prince had heard. "Indeed," he said amicably. A long-fingered hand gestured coolly toward Gideon. "He did."

Etta's gaze snapped to the man in question. Gideon stood, gaping, the note to her father held loosely in his hand. Opened.

"You read my private letter?" she accused, outraged. Had he not been in shock, she imagined he might have said it was evidence in an investigation, that it was his very duty to discover what it said. As it was, she could not help the incredulous question that came out of her instead, because she could not fathom how such a thing had happened in the first place. *"Aloud?"*

The fae prince chuckled. "Fortuitous, was it not?"

"You can't," Etta warned the prince of Gideon. "He'll not bear it." Even as she spoke, it seemed as if the man's very being had been broken, stunned into a monument by what he was witnessing like the figures that rose from the wall. But Gideon was still flesh. Gideon would have to return to Westrende. He would *know*.

The prince shrugged. "It's not for me to decide. The curse was laid upon all of us, Lady Ostwind. He'll have the sight now, same as you."

Hatred ran through Etta at the reminder and at the way he bit out her name, as if the very taste of it... well, as if he found her as distasteful as she did him. He stared back at her, not hiding that distaste in any way. *You*, his look seemed to say, *are the cause of all that has happened. Everything.* He was too spindly, his hair too long and his figure too finely dressed. He seemed to tower over her, just as he had when she'd been a girl on the floor of her room, even though a good bit of forest floor separated them and she'd grown taller. The prince was as powerful as ever, and his sharp features and finely embroidered coat seemed to scream the reminder that he was royalty. His very posture seemed to want to force her to kneel.

Her hand tightened around the grip of Gideon's sword. Etta had not forgotten what the prince had done.

"Will you not ask me of your bargain, then? What trade I would accept to return your precious life?"

Etta gave him precise directions to a dark and torturous abyss.

His jaw flexed. "Very well. Your time will run out soon

enough. Until then, I'll have my fun with your..." His gaze shifted to trail over Gideon in his uniform coat. "Oh, I see it's a chancellor. How lovely." To Etta, he spoke the aside, "Haven't collected one of those yet."

She stepped forward, sword at the ready.

"What does he mean?" Gideon's voice was level. Apparently, he'd processed at least some of what had happened. Etta couldn't be certain that was for the best.

"They've been supplanting kingdom officials," Etta said, not taking her eyes off the prince. "Lord Barrett was killed so that the painter could be replaced with a fae. To curse me and —" To the prince, she asked, "What? Why come for me when I had not yet been installed as marshal?"

A hum purred in the prince's throat. "If you do not know the answer to that, then mayhap you shouldn't have been vying for the position after all." He *tsked*. "A competent marshal would have figured us out ages ago, would they not have?"

CHAPTER 20

Etta rushed the fae prince, sword raised to strike. She was going to drive the blade through his heart and be done with their games, once and for all. His slow suffering would gain her nothing. The prince needed to be gone as quickly as possible. It all had to end.

He didn't move to defend himself in the least but let a small smile lift the edge of his lips. Etta swung. The blade glinted.

She was knocked to the dirt with a force that took her breath. Staring up at the sky, sword jarred free of her grip and flung onto the forest floor, out of reach, she could only blink in shock. Her blade had not touched the fae, and his magic had not touched her. She'd been foiled by... saints, she could not believe it.

"What are you doing?" she roared at Gideon, who pinned her bodily to the moss in an expert grip.

A chuckle came from the prince. Gideon said nothing at all.

Etta struggled beneath him but made little progress with

anything other than sinking deeper into the soft earth at her back. The prince sauntered closer, his steps slow and easy as he took in the pair of them, candidate for marshal and uniformed chancellor tangled on the ground at his feet like a pair of wild animals. "It seems all of Westrende understands something you do not, Antonetta." He crouched a man's length away from them, forearms resting on his thighs as his gaze burned into hers. "No harm may come to the Rivenwilde prince."

She raised her head to glare at Gideon. His gaze was on hers, decidedly refusing to give it to the prince of the fae. Gideon could see him, though—she knew that. The same sight she had would have been gifted to him the moment he'd called the prince's name, the moment he'd laid eyes on the man. Gideon would know. Gideon would see Etta for who she truly was.

Gideon had still stopped her.

Her head dropped to the earth, and she uttered a groan.

"You're not going to query me," the prince said, "because you know what I will ask in trade."

Etta closed her eyes. She did know. She'd known all along. She knew something else too. The fae could do no harm to a Westrende king. It was why they had kept one from coming into power, the ancient laws only safeguarding those who held a throne.

"The choice is yours, Lady Ostwind. Give me Westrende, and I will return all that you have lost."

Heartbroken, some ignoble part of her buried deep inside wanting to scream "yes, please, anything, just bring her back," Etta told the prince of Rivenwilde, "Not even if it was naught but ash." The prince had spent the better part of her life taking everything that mattered, and he could not be trusted with the one thing she had left. "Westrende will never be yours."

"Well enough," he murmured. "I'll take it on my own." He stood, tossing a speculative gaze toward Gideon. "Should you change your mind, you know how to call me." Then he strode away, whistling as if he'd not a care in the world, the eerie tune still echoing off the trees long after he was gone.

"Get off of me," Etta complained as Gideon watched the wall—through which a man had walked—aghast. She suspected he was seeing the truth of the fabled structure, the way it writhed with magic, the forms rising from its surface as if trapped for all time. His grip loosened in his apparent shock and dismay, and she was finally able to shove him off.

He rolled to his hip beside her, and she wriggled her legs from beneath his.

"Well, you've ruined any chance I had of sneaking in. Thanks for that."

Gideon's attention snapped to hers, roaming her face with an examination so careful it made her feel too seen. She wrapped her arms over her middle. His gaze followed the motion, catching on the gauze that poked from beneath her sleeve, gauze he had beheld on Margaretta's arm only hours before.

"That's right," she muttered. "Still me. It's been me all along."

Gideon was chancellor—he would be clever enough to understand what had transpired. That didn't mean it would be easy or particularly expeditious for him to adjust.

Something shifted in the shadows of a tall oak, and she reached for the sword. "We should go. It will be dark soon."

Gideon dragged his attention from Etta to the woods, where he would be seeing—for the first time—low spiky shapes moving through the shadows with unsettling speed and all-too-eager playfulness. "What is that?" His voice was low, cautious enough to make clear he understood the danger the things posed.

Etta pushed to her feet, readying his sword. "Lesser fae."

"Lesser—" One darted from behind a tree to a bush nearer where they stood, and Gideon reached for his sword.

"No, you don't." Etta jerked it out of range. "You may spar well enough, but these creatures give no quarter. You're not about to learn how they move for the first time in a forest full of them."

Gideon pressed his palms to his eyes then blinked hard, as if he might do away with the sight if he just tried hard enough.

"You'll get used to it," she told him. Used to the sight, but not used to the truth of what he was seeing. That never got any easier. "Now, come on."

She strode forward, and Gideon hurried behind her as if he meant to catch up. With a quick dodge at the last instant, he reached around her and snatched the sword. He did not need to remind her that the weapon was his, but he did anyway. She went for him. He jerked his sword arm from her grasp, so she reached beneath his coat and wrapped her hand around the grip of his dagger. Their gazes held for one long moment before she pulled it free, and for another moment after that, but they did not speak a word.

They made it nearly an hour before the first attack. Gideon, not surprisingly, was unprepared for the unnatural way they moved. It was as if the shadows rose to life, agile forms springing from the dark hollow beneath limbs and brush in one instant then clinging to their victims' chests in another. He swung at the thing stuck to him, trying desperately to get a good strike despite that it was pinned against him, its viciously long claws sunk into fabric and flesh. Two more made their attempt, taking no interest in fighting with honor, and a larger furrier beast hovered just outside of range, his dark gaze on Etta.

She wished she had a sword.

Etta drove Gideon's dagger into a small creature that leapt at her back, rolling out of its path and toward the others that circled his feet. She came up from beneath one, getting a swipe in at its haunch, then missed the other completely. Gideon's boot knocked against a felled tree, and he stumbled, but Etta's outstretched hand reached past the creatures that clung to him just in time. He grabbed hold of her forearm, steading himself, then turned his body so the beasts were not between them. In one swift move, Etta reached around to stab the thing beneath Gideon's raised arm. It screeched and fell, then with two more swipes from Etta's blade and a wide swing of Gideon's sword, the lot of them darted away to regroup with the others in the trees.

Gideon's gaze had followed, and it stayed on the larger beast as it stilled to stare back at him. He and Etta stood, pressed together. When night fell, the forest would come alive, breathing with ill intent, its magic more free in the darkness. If they didn't make it out before then, that hulking thing would be the least of their worries.

"Keeping your distance is key," Etta told him. "Once they're on you, they're too fast and wily to fight."

Gideon stared into the trees, his chest heaving. Wordlessly, he handed Etta his sword.

Her breath came too quickly, in something of a laugh. She passed him the dagger. "Come on. If we don't give them a chance, it raises ours."

"We've already passed this section of forest," Gideon said hours later.

Etta shook her head. "I know how to get us out of here. We can't turn around now."

"Night will fall soon. We need to stop and get our bearings. This cannot be right."

She frowned. It was far later than she liked, but they'd no choice but to go on. "Trust me."

"Trust you? You've done nothing but lie to me from the start."

"Of course I lied to you." She gestured wildly in an attempt to encompass all that had gone wrong. The gesture fell sadly short. "As if you would have accepted any form of the truth."

He could not argue that, despite how clearly he wanted to.

"My apologies that you feel betrayed. It's not as if you haven't called me unfit for office, accused me of a crime I didn't commit, of being a fraud, of being a spy... shall I go on?"

"I was going to have you arrested."

Her gaze snapped to his. "Me and my father both."

Gideon's mouth went hard.

"Right," she said. "Because you still may arrest him."

"You handed me evidence against him."

Etta's own mouth tightened. Her evidence wasn't all Gideon had. There was only one reason he would have possessed her father's signet ring.

They walked in silence for a long moment, their attention on the forest.

"What deal did you make with the fae?"

Etta stopped to face him, her grip tightening on the sword. "None. They set a curse upon me. I gained nothing from it." At his look, she relented. "I have made trades. The last, you saw. The painter who appeared as Lord Barrett. I gave his own name to escape my father's guard." She waved a hand dismissively. "He wasn't meant to drag you along. Before that, I traded another his life in exchange for the painter's true name. That's all."

"That's all," he repeated incredulously. "Only a few trades with the fae and some... existing relationship with the prince of Rivenwilde."

Etta slapped a palm over his mouth. "Do not speak his name."

Gideon narrowed his eyes on her. He reached up, closed his fingers slowly about her wrist, and drew the palm from his lips. They stared at each other.

Something squawked in the trees, too near.

"Go," she told Gideon, and he did, keeping hold of her as they ran.

COVERED in scratches beneath tattered clothes, they came out of the trees just as the sun dipped beneath the horizon. It was fully dark by the time Etta had led Gideon along the routes she'd learned as a girl. He'd given her a speaking look at her ability to bypass castle security, but after she'd saved him from being trapped in the greenwood overnight, he likely would have followed her anywhere.

Once they were inside the castle, Gideon seemed to become aware that their hair was woven with twigs and their clothes shredded to rags.

"Jules is going to murder me," Etta grumbled when she saw him looking. "It will be refreshing for someone pleasant to try for once."

"We can't be seen like this." His words were quiet as his gaze darted around the corridor.

Etta crossed her arms. "You mean you can't. Because it

would be unseemly for one of your station." She pointed toward her face. "I'm just a lowly assistant. I'll be fine."

"You won't be fine. You're a fugitive by now, and I at the very least will be wanted for questioning." His worried gaze snagged on a shadow in a doorway down the hall. He rubbed his eyes. "Tell me that's a dog."

"I thought you wanted me to stop lying."

Gideon pressed his eyes closed hard. He sounded a little sick. "How many of them are running around the castle?"

She made a face as she considered whether her breaking it to him there or his finding out on his own would be worse.

Gideon watched her, seeming to take in the direness of the situation for a moment before his expression shifted to into pure mortification. "Is Clara..."

Etta patted his shoulder. "No. She's just habitually wet and unwieldy. But don't trust any that you do not know. Sometimes, if the light is right, they'll catch you off guard."

"This is why—that first day in the chancery, when she leapt on you unsuspecting..." A tremor ran through him, not unlike the shaking Etta had done.

"I'd like to tell you it will get easier. But it won't."

The sound of approaching footsteps echoed down the corridor, and Gideon pulled Etta with him into a darkened alcove. "We can't walk into the chancery like this. Not when the kingsmen were chasing us hours ago."

It had been a bit more than a few hours, and her father had likely posted kingsmen at the chancery entrance, but Etta didn't have the energy to quibble. Instead, she let him lead her through the lesser-used corridors to the courtyard that connected to his rooms.

As he closed the door behind them, he took her hand, guiding her through the darkness to a small study where he placed her atop a settee. She could barely make out his form as he moved through the windowless room, his steps sure in the familiar space. He lit a candle then placed it on a table to retrieve two more. The room came to light to reveal rich polished wood, close walls lined with bookshelves, a small desk, and only the one settee. He moved one candle to the table beside her then the other two opposite the settee. Shrugging out of his ruined coat, he gestured that she wait.

Etta leaned against the cushions with a sigh, kicking off her slippers and vowing never to wear anything but boots until the fae were no longer in existence. She was too tired to go through his things, despite that a fine inlaid box atop his desk promised to hold something interesting and the many books on the side table would reveal what he read in his private hours. She loosened the tie of her dress, just a little, and found a gaping hole down the side. She would have to burn the whole thing before Jules found it.

Gideon returned with a basin and pitcher in one hand, a plate of food in the other, and a bundle of supplies beneath his arm. He spread them out on a low table then scooted it closer to the settee.

Apparently having washed as he retrieved the basin, his shirt sleeves were rolled up to reveal clean forearms and hands. Etta took the soap from him to begin on her own while Gideon retrieved a decanter of water and a finely made cup. Once filled, he held it up.

"I've only the one."

Etta could not be made to care. She dried her hands, drank deeply, then handed the cup back, brushing off her nails and rinsing her arms a second time before drinking again. Gideon had collapsed onto the cushions by then with rye bread and a piece of fruit. When the nectar dribbled into his wounds, he leaned forward to wipe them on a towel.

"Here," Etta said, taking his arm to examine the cuts. "Those need tending."

He tugged it back. "You don't have to."

She drew it to her again. "I do. Elsewise, you'll have to explain them to someone." She turned his palm over, tracing a fingertip up the inside of his forearm with a wince. They did not look pleasant. Leaving his hand resting on her thigh, she leaned forward to riffle through the supplies he'd brought in. Setting several ointments and tonics aside, she chose a small amber pot of salve.

"They'll only burn the first few days," she told him. "But make sure you keep them clean. They've a bad habit of carrying on unless they're tended well."

He watched her, sleeves tugged up to her elbows, carefully applying salve to each of his wounds. "How are you not covered in thousands of these?"

A humorless laugh escaped her. "I learned early." She glanced up at him. "I was very young when I first saw the prince. It seemed to incite something in his beasts whenever I looked at them. I don't recall being attacked once before I saw them for what they truly were. Once I did, though, they were relentless."

"It's part of the curse," Gideon murmured as if remembering what the fae prince had said.

He flinched when she touched a particularly deep cut, and she leaned closer, examining the wound to be certain nothing remained inside. "He calls it a curse. We call it the Rive. The thing that binds the fae, that holds them beyond the wall... it keeps us from seeing them as they truly are."

"Until we set eyes on the prince."

Etta nodded. "Only him. The book we took from my father's vault says the thrones of the Riven Court and that of Westrende were tied in the bargain that created the Rive. It's my belief that the protections he's afforded, the edict that the prince of the fae must not be harmed"—the brief look she shot him was only partially an accusation for what he'd done in the clearing— "is why whatever keeps the others from seeing falls away in his presence. We must know it is him. We have to be given the chance to see the truth." Lest a misstep be made.

"I am not sorry for stopping you," he said of Etta's attempt at skewering the prince. "But I confess, when I opened your letter, it was as if the word called for me to speak it. It was not my intent and I do not do such things, not here."

He was right. Etta had sat across from him in his office for days. He'd never read aloud from anything that had crossed his desk. She shrugged. "I likely would never have made it back through in any case. Desperation rarely leads to success."

Gideon blinked. "You were going through the wall."

"I told you as much."

He swallowed. "I didn't think... I mean, of course I understood that someone might get through. I was aware there was a process of sorts. But I didn't—I don't think I ever believed. Truly." He gave her his gaze. "I would have stopped you."

Etta grinned. "You would have tried."

"Saints," he breathed. "This explains why my new assistant was so good with a sword."

The reminder settled unpleasantly upon Etta's whole being. The curse would end soon. It was time to accept that it was over, that she'd lost her chance and would need either to surrender to it or find someplace to hide until the apple rotted through. Every comfort she'd found since her return would be stolen once more. "I suppose there's no point in returning to Margaretta now."

"I don't know," he said quietly. "Her company was growing on me."

The statement threw Etta so off balance that she stared openly at him.

Glancing up at her through his dark lashes and with a

flash of that boyish grin sneaking over his lips, he said, "And Clara seems to enjoy her company a great deal."

Heat swelled in Etta's chest at the timbre of his voice, and she became abruptly aware that she'd been sliding a thumb idly over the skin inside his wrist. She snatched her hand back from his. "Gideon, when I'm gone, there will be no one else who knows. And if you... if it turns out my father..." If the general was guilty of making bargains with the fae...

Gideon reached to take her hand in his, a gesture more comforting than it had been before.

She stared at their intertwined hands where they rested atop their touching knees. She had to tell him. "It was my fault," she said.

"What was your fault?"

She swallowed the lump in her throat. "The first time. When he came for my mother."

Gideon went still. His strong hand remained cradling hers, but she suddenly felt more distance. The shame in Etta's words made the hedged confession clear. Gideon was sharp enough to fill in the rest from their encounter with the fae.

His voice was low. "The prince killed your mother? The general said she was taken by illness. There was a record of it —the entire family isolated for months to prevent its spread. She suffered a great deal. He told me himself."

Etta met his gaze. "She's not dead."

Everything about Gideon's posture seemed to want to bolt to standing, to act on her words. But he held himself there, keeping her hand in his, his thoughts surely recalling every word he'd heard spoken by the general in all the years of their acquaintance and by the fae prince earlier that very day.

"He has her," Gideon said numbly. "He offered to break your curse and to return everything he'd taken from you."

"He has her because of me. I spoke his name. I called him there. She made the trade to keep me safe. The prince thought to take the general's daughter but instead won an official of the kingdom who was also the general's wife."

Gideon's brows shifted. "But you were only a girl." At her tortured expression, he added, "How could you have known?"

Etta pulled her hand from his. "It doesn't matter that I didn't know what would happen. I did it. I caused this. Without my recklessness, she never would have gone. She traded her own safety for mine." It had been horrific. Her mother had made Etta swear never to call the prince and never to come for her, lest the sacrifice be in vain. Etta was to become marshal. She was to grow into the woman who would defeat the prince on his throne, who would do the one thing her father had not.

Etta had failed them all.

"No." Gideon placed a finger beneath her chin to drag her gaze to his. "I mean, how could you have known his name?"

Etta stared at him, opened her mouth to speak, then caught the words. She'd no idea. She had never thought of it. At that age, Etta hadn't the wherewithal to assign blame.

Blame came later and not for anyone but herself and maybe her father, because he had made her hide the truth.

"Antonetta." The word came as natural as any that had slipped off Gideon's tongue, despite how it rumbled through her. "Someone gave you that name. Someone placed it in your hands. The hands of a child."

The same name that had been drawn from a chancellor as if against his will. She'd never considered that the fault may not have been entirely hers to bear. After a moment of stunned silence, Etta said, "Perhaps the prince was right. Perhaps I am not shrewd enough for the position of marshal."

Gideon shifted closer, intensely focusing on her face. He would have been able to see both the truth and the lie, now, the same as she. It was impossible to know which he was after. "You're not telling me everything about the curse. They took something from you. What was it?"

Etta explained what had happened with Lord Barrett, the terms Elsher had left her with, and the details he'd left out.

That the fae had stolen her life.

Gideon Alexander straightened at the words *the painting for your life* then dropped her hands, stood, and strode from the room.

CHAPTER 21

I t had to have been past midnight. The chancery was
dark. Not a single sound echoed through the chamber.
Gideon moved with the grace of a man who could
traverse the entire wing in a blindfold—Etta, not so much.
She stumbled behind him, trying desperately not to make a
sound and to stay at his heels. They were fugitives, after all.
The last thing she needed was to get caught.

Her stomach dropped when they came into the records
room. Moonlight cast the floor in strips of blue. A candle
flared to life at Gideon's hand, illuminating the determination
on his face and casting the room in a warmer tone. As she
walked farther into the room, his light revealed the thing that
had filled Etta with dread.

She wanted to stop him, to prevent him from seeing.
Gideon had encountered the prince. He'd gained true sight.
He would be able to take in every horrid detail.

He reached up and tugged the drape to drop to the floor.
Standing in the dim light before Etta's portrait, holding the
single taper aloft, Gideon was transfixed. Etta watched him,

the painting and his figure illuminated in the center of a space whose edges fell to shadows and darkness.

Whatever Gideon's thoughts, he did not seem to find the portrait ridiculous. Instead, he appeared to examine with great concern the rotting apple perched delicately in her painted hands. His eyes did not stay long on the carnival behind her, lingering mostly on her image. His attention snagged on the ribbon laced through her lips and, as if the magic drew him closer, Gideon raised his hand to hover above the canvas. His fingertip grazed lightly over the ribbon on her likeness's painted lips, and Etta shivered at the touch.

Gideon clearly felt it, as he turned his face to hers and let his gaze fall to her mouth. He stared for an interminably long moment. Something seemed to come to him, and he glanced at the portrait—specifically the slit in the canvas—then back to Etta's wounded arm.

He went entirely still.

Indeed, Etta thought. No part of what he was realizing was good. The curse had hold of her, and it had nothing but ill intent.

His expression shifted, the change evident even in the light of a single candle. Etta's stomach flipped again.

"You're giving me that look," she said.

His voice was rough. "What look?"

"You think I'm a misfit. One of those souls you'd sacrifice everything to help." Like the ones he'd gathered to chancery, like Etta herself that first day, shaken and bedraggled and begging for a post.

He held her gaze. "They're not misfits. They're exceptional."

Etta swallowed. "But you're going to help me, whether I ask for it or not."

He turned back to the canvas then set the candle aside to reverently lower the drape and cover the cursed portrait from view. When he finally faced Etta again, it was with the most solemn expression she'd ever seen. He sighed, unapologetic. "I'm afraid it's a flaw in my character."

Etta's chest heaved in something painfully close to a sob. She did not cry out but only stood there, silent as Gideon moved to draw her into his arms.

One of his hands wrapped gently to the curve at the back of her neck, his other lower, keeping her close.

When the emotion seizing her chest melted into something less painful, Etta raised her chin to look at him. "Gideon?" she asked. "Would it be a great crime against the dignity of the chancery office if you were to kiss someone recently on staff?"

He was unbearably near, his answer a soft breath that brushed her lips. "Yes," he said, drifting almost imperceptibly nearer. "A very, very great—"

Etta grabbed the front of his shirt, yanked him to close the distance, and kissed him full on the mouth. Gideon made no hesitation, walking them back to press Etta against the stacks, sliding his hands beneath her arms to lift her the short distance to his height and deepen the kiss. He was relentless, not breaking the contact even as Etta's roving hand knocked the book tucked in the back of his waistband to the floor. A little growl sounded deep in his throat, as if he could not help it, sending warmth through Etta's entire being. She kept one hand still knotted in his shirtfront, refusing to let go, lest he come to his senses and attempt escape. She tilted her head, unable to get close enough, and Gideon shifted to meet her, his palm sliding over her thigh to bring them closer still.

Footsteps sounded outside. Gideon froze. Etta took a heartbeat longer to regain awareness of their situation. The pair of them hung there for a moment in the flickering light of a single candle, motionless, listening.

The night patrol, Etta thought numbly, remembering the

muffled thump the book had made when it dropped to the floor. *They heard and are coming to investigate. Gideon will send them away. It will be fine.*

Gideon lowered Etta to the ground, shifting in front of her as he purposefully slid the book beneath a shelf with his boot. They were trapped with nowhere to hide and no exit aside from the door through which they'd entered. He would have to think of an excuse for whatever they were about, the chancellor and his assistant, alone in a dark records room in the small hours before dawn. But it would be all right.

The footfalls neared, and Gideon's gaze flicked toward the portrait. A heartbeat later, he was moving toward the door.

He didn't make it. Two kingsmen blocked the entrance, shouldering inside with a half dozen more at their backs.

They were not chancery patrol. They were her father's men, the private guard of General Ostwind. Etta stepped backward, but there was nowhere to go.

The kingsmen didn't wait. They shoved past Gideon, and the first two snatched hold of Etta by the arms as the others pressed Gideon back from the door. When they lined the small room, a new figure came into view.

The General of Westrende stood in the doorway, his hard stare on Etta's face and form. The kingsmen passed a light forward, and the man near Etta held it high to illuminate her face. Whatever work the glamour was doing, her father knew well enough that not being able to recall his intruder's description, even as he looked directly at it, would mean she was somehow connected to the fae and that she was guilty of being in his rooms.

"That's her." His voice was cold, his expression colder. "Take her." The general's gaze flicked to Gideon. "And you, I'll see stood before council for harboring a fugitive, before the week is done."

Gideon's face had gone hard, the stern, sharp jaw of chancellor back in place. Etta jerked against the soldiers' grip, despite having no chance to defeat eight armed men and her father with nothing more than her fists. Her father would refuse to believe it was Etta—he could only accept that it was a fae trick, that his daughter was gone forever like her mother. "Take me where?"

The first sign of pleasure crossed the general's expression. "To a cell for what's left of the night. But soon, before council, where you'll be tried for treason."

CHAPTER 22

Prisoners of Westrende, it turned out, had no ranking. They were placed in cells in the order in which they'd been arrested. It meant a high-born lord, despite his status and attachment to sundry comforts, could be settled next to a lowly, filth-covered lady of treasonous intent. And it was how the girl previously known as Margaretta was tossed to the damp stone floor of a cool, dim cell next to Nickolas Brigham of the venerable Brigham line.

"Sometimes, in my nightmares, we're attacked by birds," Nickolas said dourly, shoving his arms through the bars so that they dangled into Etta's cell. "And at the end, our clothes look precisely like that dress."

Etta gasped. "Nickolas."

He sighed. "I suppose I knew it was coming. The general's spies spotted us meeting outside the chancery, searched my rooms, and found a stack of parchment concealed beneath my closet floor that apparently detailed closely held state secrets. I can't say for certain because I was never allowed to read them."

Etta groaned. She had not thought she could feel more

wretched. "I'll tell them," she vowed. "I swear to you, I will clear your name."

He gave her a level look. "I beg of you, do not do me any more favors. The last thing I need is a treasonous lady with no trace of papers or connections taking up my cause." He frowned. "Are you well? You look miserable, but I don't see any open wounds."

She scooted closer to the bars. Her wrists were pinned in irons, so there was little chance she would be able to wriggle free. "They haven't hurt me yet, but my father is certainly out for blood. First, he caught Margaretta in his office, spying. Then more recently, someone with a similar face broke into his private vault."

Nickolas drew back and took a long breath. "His vault. I have to say, my lady, I did not think you could surprise me." His tone implied the "but here we are."

Etta bit her lip.

"Saints." Nickolas moaned. "There's more?"

"I was being chased, so... well, it didn't seem I had any other choice." She let him have her gaze. "I called a fae to bargain my escape. We disappeared right before the kings-men's eyes."

"We," Nickolas said slowly.

Etta cleared her throat. "The chancellor and me."

Nickolas was silent for so long that she began to wonder if he'd heard her.

"I was trying to cross the wall without calling the prince—"

"Calling the prince." Nickolas, apparently snapped back to life by insuppressible incredulity, drew his arms back to grip hold of the bars. "You possess the true name of the prince of Rivenwilde?" When Etta only stared back at him, his tone shifted into something more sardonic. "Oh, truly, and why

have you just not spoken it all along? Why not call him for tea? Why not have him over for a game of—"

"Nickolas," Etta said calmly. "You seem overset."

"Overset," he repeated with considerable outrage. "Antonetta, you have just seen us—though honestly, I cannot fathom why this comes as a surprise—but you have seen us thrown into a pair of prison cells fit for the lowest of the kingdom's most criminal kind, admitted to bargaining with a fae *while* you are wearing his curse, no less, to revealing all of this to a chancellor who wants you thrown from office before you even take your post, and then casually mention that you might call on the prince of the Riven Court." He glared at her. "Do go on about my delicate emotional state."

"Point taken."

His forehead thunked against the iron bars. "You're not going to get out of this one, are you?"

Her throat felt thick. "No. I won't."

When his eyes rose to hers, they held a question: *won't, not can't?*

Antonetta Ostwind possessed the true name of a fae. She could bargain her way out of anything.

Etta's gaze dropped to her lap, wrists bound and hands limp upon the tattered fabric of a borrowed dress. Her voice was barely above a whisper when she said, "No matter how I might want it, the cost is too high."

CHAPTER 23

Etta stood before the long table where she had, only weeks before, looked on with a heart swollen with hope and pride. The council chamber in all its majesty felt hollow despite the twelve kingdom officials seated at the table's sides.

Her arms were heavy, the manacles at her wrists seeming to weigh even on her soul. Every gaze in the chamber had skimmed over the face she wore, not meeting the familiar bright eyes they'd known since she was a girl.

Not even her father, who should have, above anyone, recognized them as easily as his own. The general stared back at Etta, radiating pure loathing.

"Ostwind," Louis demanded of the general, "why have you called us here for this scrap of a girl?"

"Treason." He gestured to an assistant, who rushed forward to deliver documents to several heads of law and kingdom order. "Conspiring against the kingdom, assuming a fake identity to gain sensitive information regarding the prospects for king, acting against a kingdom official with ill intent"—he waved a hand toward the document— "the list goes on."

Etta noted that he did not mention how she'd broken into his rooms. She gave him a look she hoped would convey that she was onto him. Etta had information he would not want revealed. He had no way of knowing she no longer possessed his book, a surely outlawed collection of pages that detailed the laws of fae magic.

They'd searched her. They'd searched her rooms. The general had found nothing.

His gaze stayed on hers. "The most pressing point," he noted, "is that she evaded capture by way of magic."

Cerys's tone was hard. "Consorting with the fae?"

Stefan's usually warm eyes narrowed on Etta with open disdain. "You think she wears a glamour. That she's one of them."

The general gestured toward Etta. "Decide for yourself. Look away and see that you might list one single attribute once she's out of your sight."

"I have your eyes," Etta murmured. "There's an attribute for you."

The general's hand dropped to the table in a manner so controlled it was more threatening than if he'd slammed a fist. He would remember what she'd said in his office, that she was his daughter, that she was truly Antonetta. He did not believe her. He had decided she was just another fae trickery, one of the like they'd used on him before. "Another word, and you'll be gagged."

"I invoke prisoner's rights."

His tone was level. "You have no rights. You are not a citizen of Westrende."

The council members watching Etta turned their attention to the general.

"What do you want to do with her?" Cerys asked.

General Ostwind's gaze met the cursed magic he'd hated for so long, obscuring Etta's face. His voice held the hint of the satisfaction of a game won. "A filigree cage."

Etta felt as though she'd been struck hard in the chest. Her knees went weak and her heart wild. He had never meant to stick her in a cell, to let her slowly fade in the darkness of a Westrende prison. He meant to bind her inside the magic that made up the wall, a tracery of metal that kept anything fae from passing through. She had been wrong. Her father never could have been guilty of making deals with the fae. He hated them too deeply.

In a filigree cage, she would not linger until her curse came to an end then be spirited away to Rivenwilde. She would be trapped, unable to fulfill the terms of the curse and unable to break free. The flesh would rot on her bones, like the withering apple her likeness held in the portrait. She would be trapped forever inside a curse, neither living nor dead.

The prince would not have his due.

Bile rose from Etta's stomach. Saints, she was going to be sick right there in the council chamber.

Gideon's sentiment that she must have been given the prince's name by someone when she was a girl came back to her. She recalled the dark days that followed, too, with her mother gone and her father severe. *Do not speak their name*, he'd told her. *Speak of them and they will return.*

Next time, he'd told her, *they will take something worse than just you.*

She wanted so badly to scream it at the top of her lungs, to shriek the prince's name to the sky, anything at all to see her mother returned and to see herself set free despite the vow to her mother and the warnings from her father. But she could not—would not. The price was too high.

She met his gaze. "You say a filigree cage yet deny the

existence of fae. The public face of Westrende is no less a glamour than what covers my own." She jerked her chin toward the council. "This is all an illusion. The fae threaten our very lives, you know it, and yet you remain. Your silence keeps nothing at bay. The prince is coming, and he means to unrend the world, to break the Rive. And when he does, Westrende will have nothing to save it while you cling to your silence. But I will not give you to him, not even if you deserve the fate more than she."

"Silence!" The general stood, his voice like thunder, his anger like the coming storm.

Etta had no way of knowing whether he understood her words, but he would know soon enough. The prince wanted to break the curse that kept fae from Westrende, and to do so, he needed power over the kingdom. Controlling the general was the closest he could come.

"I call the vote," her father said. "Speak your objections now, for this creature belongs in a cage, and I mean to see it done before the hour is through."

Etta had no more than resigned herself to her fate when the doors to the council chamber banged open. Cerys froze, gavel in hand, only a breath before the mallet met its base to settle the course of Etta's doom.

All eyes turned toward the chamber door as Gideon Alexander strode in.

"Stop him," the general growled. "This is a private trial, and he is connected to the suspect's crime. He shall not be allowed to interfere with this proceeding."

Gideon's steps did not slow even as the kingsmen approached. "I am still chancellor." The calm in his voice was not as level as one might have expected, but Etta could not say whether that owed to the fact that her father meant to arrest him or that he was clearly about to declare something utterly ridiculous in Etta's defense.

Cold dread rose in her, and she prayed he would not attempt to convince the rule of twelve that the fae walked among them, that they gathered outside those very chambers. The council would not tolerate those who spoke freely of the fae and certainly not those who challenged their judgment. Etta had only spoken openly because she was already doomed.

Gideon did not give the general his notice but let his gaze travel the table of men and women who made up Westrende's rule. "Will you deny me the right to submit evidence?"

Louis gestured the kingsmen away. "Lord Alexander is welcome, should he have anything of value to provide."

"I do." Gideon's tone had strengthened, but his gaze never strayed to Etta or her father. It was good, she supposed, that he did not look at her, because she would not have been able to stop herself from frantically waving at him to run away—or worse, that he might show her kindness and cause her to weep in front of everyone present.

He stopped, apparently undecided where to stand, given that the table was occupied on every side, with Etta at one end and her father at the other. One of Gideon's hands was pressed to his midsection, and Etta had a sudden wave of fear that he might be about to reveal the book, that it was hidden beneath his robe and he intended to bring it forth—as evidence against her father. The one person left to defend Westrende against the prince would be thereby removed from his post. It felt a bit like she was standing aboard a ship, with the floor beneath her feet swaying unsteadily.

"I have," Gideon started, still not looking at her. "I have evidence—" He stopped, the hand not pressed to his middle coming up to wipe sweat from his brow. Beneath his breath, he murmured something that sounded a lot like "fates protect us." He let the council have his gaze. "Forgive me for what I'm about to do."

The swaying ship deck beneath Etta's feet plunged into the ocean. She was certain by his tone that he was about to commit an act far worse than presenting evidence against her father. Gideon was going to do something that would cost him more than even his own post. She shouted, "Gideon, no!"

He did not heed her. Instead, Gideon Alexander, chancellor of Westrende and most law-abiding citizen in the history of histories, moved to the center of the council chamber and spoke the prince's name.

CHAPTER 24

Etta stared in shock at the prince of Rivenwilde, who stood in the center of the highest office of Westrende, surrounded by gaping council leaders. He was perched atop their hallowed table, looking down at his oldest enemies as the ancient magic revealed to them the sight.

Cerys cursed, Maura drew a sword, and Louis shoved up from his chair so hard that it crashed to the floor. There was a lot to be said about the amount of force it took, for they were not insignificant chairs.

"Well," the prince said with a careless grin toward Gideon. "Look what you have done."

The fae wore a long-tailed suit of solid black, silky and sleek, fit perfectly to him. Upon his head was a tangled crown of bonelike spikes that rested tidily in a nest of neat dark hair. Every detail on his person was perfectly done, as if he'd dressed for the occasion.

Etta's gaze swung to Gideon, his drab robe and mildly sick expression a stark contrast to the prince's flair. He had done the thing that Etta had never been able to do, the thing her father had threatened her about and that her mother had made her swear never to do. The council could see.

"Gideon," she said breathily, unsure if he understood precisely what he'd done, how he'd tied them all into the dark secret that the prince called a curse. At the sound of her voice, though, eyes turned to Etta, and three more council members shoved out of their chairs.

"You see," Gideon said evenly. "Now that you've encountered the prince, you see what he has done. Lady Ostwind is not guilty. She was acting in the best interest of Westrende, despite being constrained by a curse."

The prince chuckled. "Oh, indeed. Poor Lady Ostwind." He snapped his wrist, and suddenly, a sword was in his hand, which he casually spun so that light flashed on its blade. "As if it were not I who is truly bound."

There was too much happening. Etta could not quite decide where to look. "Cut me free," she murmured to Maura. She settled her gaze on her father at the opposite end of the table, seemingly leagues away with the prince between them.

"Antonetta," her father whispered.

"I know," she replied. She knew he hadn't been able to accept it was her. She knew he was sorry. She understood that his biggest fear had come to life. "There's nothing to be done for it."

"I only wanted—" He stopped, appearing speechless, which Etta was sure she'd never seen. The general swallowed hard, and his voice was rough when he spoke. "I tried to keep you safe."

It was as if Etta's heart had been run through the wash, wrung out, and pinned to the line. She could do nothing but wait until it resumed any shape that was normal. She could not think about what it all meant. Perhaps, he hadn't sent her away to be rid of her but because she mattered too much. Perhaps he couldn't bear to lose her too.

"Heartwarming," the prince said flatly. He glanced at Etta. "Now, what's going on? He was about to pin you in a cage?"

She glared up at him.

"Best leave it," he told Maura, who was fumbling with the locks of Etta's manacles. "If she gets free, she'll have a sword before you know it, and she'll attempt to break the oldest covenant among a long, long list of rules never to be broken" —he shot Etta a look—"again."

Pinning the sword to his side, he loudly clapped his hands once, calling the assembled crowd to order as he faced Gideon. "Let's get to it, shall we? What sort of bargain do you propose?"

"Lift the curse from Antonetta Ostwind."

The prince's smile was slow.

Gideon reached into his robe to withdraw the book. "And call her mother to bear witness."

Etta's knees gave out. She barely caught herself on the edge of the table, gouging the wood with her manacles. It was not her proudest moment. Across the room, her father made some sort of incoherent cry, apparently not faring much better.

Gideon held the book before him like a talisman. "It must be allowed, per Riven Court law."

Saints, he'd read it and had already researched the rules by which the prince must behave. He did seem a bit bedraggled, now that she looked, as if, like her, he'd been up through the night. But Gideon wasn't a prisoner. He had not been in a cell next to Nickolas, knowing his last hours were slipping past. He was chancellor, diligent and meticulous, knowledgeable in nothing so much as the law. He had stayed up pouring over fae rules.

Bless the man's studious soul.

The prince crouched on the table to meet Gideon's confident gaze. "Are you certain you want to play this game?"

"Call her," Gideon said, "by the rules of your code."

The prince's answering tone implied that he was humoring Gideon, as if he'd no other occupation for the day other than to watch how it all played out and that he had no care for the laws that bound him. "So be it."

Gideon moved forward, drawing strips of paper from inside his robe to hand to Cerys and Louis. "As you'll see, Lady Ostwind has committed none of the crimes of which she's been accused. She was acting on behalf of the chancery, pursuing the very task she was assigned in order that her nomination be allowed to return to vote."

He paused as if just realizing that Etta *had* completed his task. The fae had supplanted agents of the kingdom and had meddled in every manner possible relating to the head of Westrende. She had uncovered precisely who'd made attempts on the prospects for king—she just hadn't been able to tell anyone. Because no one would have believed her. He paused as if realizing that she had planned to fight the fae on her own.

"Indeed," Gideon told the council, his gaze caught on Etta's. "I vouch for the lady's character and the very Ostwind name."

Maura seemed distraught that the focus was being drawn away from the very tall, very fae figure atop their table. "The office of marshal is the least of our problems at the moment. Lord Alexander, what are you about?"

Papers delivered, Gideon stepped back, his hands clasped before his waist, where they held the book of fae law. "In fact, my lady, the office of marshal is very much to the point." He let the prince have his gaze. "Rivenwilde has been positioning fae among us, in posts near officers of the kingdom. Their most ardent desire, it seems, is to possess the seat of power. Lacking a king, that position falls to the head of council."

Every gaze in the room, save Gideon and the prince,

turned toward the general. He sank into his chair. Etta had not yet reclaimed her heart—she would have to decide later whether she held sympathy for the fact that the secrets the man had so desperately clung to were unraveling before his eyes. As it was, she could not quite grasp the relief she'd anticipated of having it finally out. The council could no longer deny the existence of fae in Westrende, not with their prince strutting before them. And yet, nothing could be done to stop the consequences of it all coming undone.

The lock of the irons at Etta's wrists finally clicked free, and Maura removed them and took one of the papers that had been silently passed through the room. Etta rubbed her flesh. Her fingers itched for a weapon, but Gideon had been correct. She could not run the prince through. What they needed was a filigree cage.

But before Etta could signal her father to set up a trap, his expression melted into something Etta might never have seen. *Might*, she thought, because somewhere, far off in her memory, was the shadow of the same emotion crossing her father's face. When he had discovered they'd taken...

"Marianna." The general's voice was a plea, as if he could not quite believe it was true.

But it was true, and Etta could see it. Atop the long table beside the prince of Rivenwilde, her mother, the lady Ostwind, who'd been stolen when Etta was only a girl, suddenly stood. The same Lady Ostwind the council believed to be dead.

The council members stumbled away from the table—all eleven, save her father—just as Etta tried to climb aboard. Maura and Stefan dragged Etta backward, as if she were the danger. Perhaps she was, she thought, as the prince smiled down at her.

No harm could come to a prince of Rivenwilde, no harm to one who held the throne. The prince believed he was cursed. He blamed Etta for what had become of her mother. He'd said as much when Etta had called his name.

"Lady Ostwind." Gideon bowed deeply toward Etta's mother, as if the room had not broken into utter chaos around him. "You have been called to bear witness. A curse has been laid upon Antonetta, but she has refused to ask the prince for a bargain to win herself free. Today, I will bargain for her, in hopes that what I offer will be valuable enough to return our incoming marshal to fight another day."

Restrained by Stefan and Maura, Etta watched her mother take in the man in chancellor's robes, telling her the prince had cursed her daughter, seeding important hints to their situation into a succinct introduction, and the council members, who appeared as if they'd seen her rise from the dead. Her gaze moved toward Etta, softening with warm affection and pride, bright with unshed tears as her lips shifted into something of a smile. Then, quite deliberately, her focus moved to the other end of the table, where her husband still stood.

There was a frozen moment in which Etta could see nothing but her father's answering expression, the torture and awe melting into steely determination, as if he meant to ride into battle.

Etta's knees felt weak. "Let me go." The two holding her did not listen.

"Bear witness, I will," Marianna said. "But first, I offer a trade of my own."

CHAPTER 25

"No!" Etta shouted just as the prince rammed his blade into the table with a crash of magic, driving a hush through the watching crowd.

Into the silence, the prince said, "There is only one trade I might accept from you, Marianna. Do you offer it now, after so many years of refusal?"

Etta's mother seemed to hesitate, her throat moving in a swallow, her gaze flicking briefly to the general then to Gideon before finally stopping on Etta once more.

"Take me," Etta pled to the fae. "It's what you wanted. Have me and leave them alone."

The prince flicked a hand as if swatting at an insect. "I have a bigger prize in mind, Lady Ostwind." He'd not even looked at her, his focus solely on Etta's mother. They all knew what he wanted, what he'd wanted all along.

The head of Westrende.

Etta's mother was going to give it to him. Marianna's shoulders squared, the simple gray gown she wore somehow suddenly regal. Her amber eyes shifted toward the prince. "I offer, in exchange for my own freedom and for a reprieve of one year in which you vow to never cross the border into Westrende..."

The entire room fell under a disbelieving pall, the gravity of Marianna's words impossible. The future of Westrende hung on the final utterance from a woman they'd thought they would never see in the flesh again and who was about to give it all away.

"My husband, general of Westrende."

The prince had wanted him all along. Etta had refused to be any part of giving him over, though, because her mother had made her swear a vow and her father had threatened to send her away.

Giving him over meant the end of the kingdom.

Etta jerked free, Gideon rushed forward, and nearly every member of the council drew their weapons.

In one instant, the prince raised a hand, triumphantly calling, "Done."

In the next, Etta became aware of the bang that had preceded his decree. It seemed to echo through the chamber.

The prince's gaze fell to Cerys, her hoary eyes on him as a wicked smiled crossed her lips. In one hand, she held the gavel. In the other, the strip of parchment Gideon had given her when he'd first come in, a paper that Etta had believed had detailed her innocence. Etta stared at its twin, the crumped parchment that had been passed to Maura moments before—a parchment, she saw, that had warned of a coming threat.

It asked the council to remove the general before Westrende was taken.

"What have you done?" The prince's voice was ice, his face twisted in fury. He lurched forward, but Etta's mother had hold of the neck of his fine jacket, and no less than half a dozen swords were abruptly aimed at his person.

"What she has done," Marianna whispered menacingly at

his back, "is release the general from his post as head of council." Marianna returned Cerys's smile. "And finely so. You always had excellent timing, my friend."

Etta's father pressed through the crowd, stopping when he was face level with the crouching prince. "You do not look pleased. You've won a general and an Ostwind. Is that not enough?"

The prince went for him, but it was too late. The bargain had been struck. The price had not won a head of the kingdom. He grabbed hold of the general's coat, jerking him forward, threats pouring from him with a good deal of oaths and swearing. Etta's father did not seem to care in the least. His attention was only for Marianna, their eyes locked as she stood atop the table, an arm's length out of his reach. What passed between them was hard to say, but Etta could see, even from where she stood, that the look held nothing but vows of duty and devotion—not simply for Westrende but for one another. And for Etta.

The prince tore free of the council members, leaping down to seize his prize. The general appeared unconcerned as his attention turned to Etta. "You have done us proud, Antonetta. Westrende could not ask for a more adept marshal."

It was the first moment for as long as she could recall that Etta cared not a whit about becoming marshal. She rushed forward, trying to reach him before the prince turned and yanked the general away from the crowd.

"Hold!" Gideon ordered.

The look the prince shot him was so filled with contempt that something in Etta wanted to shrink back.

Gideon only moved closer. "The curse."

"You think I would set her free after the betrayal you all have dealt? I would sooner cut off my own hand."

Gideon lifted the book. "You've forgotten, I know the

rules."

The prince's jaw pressed so tight that it seemed his teeth might break. "Offer."

Gideon slid the book into his belt then positioned his hands patiently before his waist. "In exchange for the breaking of Antonetta Ostwind's curse, I relinquish your true name."

The prince leaned threateningly toward Gideon.

"If you do not make this trade, I will invoke your name, and you will be drawn across the border, breaking your bargain with Lady Ostwind," Gideon said.

"It does not work that way," the prince snapped. "I may cross without repercussion if called."

The tilt to Gideon's mouth said that he'd only been testing the boundary of their rules. He'd gotten his answer. He drew a breath. "In that case, a counteroffer." He gestured toward the dozen officers of Westrende watching. "Each fae we find on our side of the boundary will be locked inside a filigree cage so that they may not assist you across. Perhaps, knowing this, you'd be willing to trade the breaking of Antonetta's curse for the return of those prisoners to Rivenwilde land, with the agreement, of course, that no additional fae pass through."

"You cannot leave them," Etta said. Without the ability to return to Rivenwilde, the fae would be starved of magic. He would be sentencing them to death. "The law says—"

"I know our own laws." The prince shot her a glare then turned back to Gideon. "The two of you will pay for what you have done." The hand not tangled in the general's coat twisted through the air, and suddenly, in it rested a fresh, bright apple. He tossed it aloft, the breaking of a curse, and vowed, "This isn't over."

By the time the apple landed in Gideon's palm, the prince —and Etta's father—were gone.

CHAPTER 26

The curse was broken. Etta had wanted desperately to win back her life. Her post as marshal. Her mother. She had not expected that it would cost so much.

But the Rive was intact. The prince was gone.

"Darling girl," Marianna said, wrapping her arms around Etta in a hug that made her want to fall to the ground and weep. Etta's mother pulled back to look at her. "I'm so sorry, my love. I'm so sorry for having gone."

Etta nodded, unable to speak past the lump in her throat.

"We'll make it right. I've learned so much while I was away. What your father gained from that book was nothing compared to what I know from being beyond the wall." She pressed her hands to Etta's cheeks. "I've so much to do. It all needs to be dealt with straight away. See me tonight, yes? Come find me once this is settled, and we'll spend hours upon hours tucked before the hearth."

Etta nodded again, turning her face to kiss her mother's palm.

Then her mother tucked a lock of hair behind Etta's ear, wholly present for a frozen moment before she smiled and rushed away. Etta watched fondly as she crossed the room, giving only a quick look back before reaching the members of council. The woman had always been a force, and that hadn't changed. Despite her years away, Marianna took hold of council as if she'd formed it from her own will. She would see everything set to rights. The lady Ostwind would take her place as the new head of council, possibly even as general, and she would see her husband returned.

The lady Ostwind would stand against the fae.

Gideon moved beside Etta and slid his hand into hers, their fingers tangling in the most natural way.

Etta let her gaze travel from face to face as the council members, who had been so adamant in their refusal to change, talked animatedly with her mother. Etta would no longer be forced to stand alone in her fight against the fae. They had the sight, so council could not deny the existence of the creatures. And she was not alone because Gideon would stand with her. They'd created a world where it might be possible to root out the fae, together. She turned to him, closer than propriety might have permitted.

His gaze roamed her face. The curse was broken, and nothing but Antonetta remained. The breath that came out of him was one only of relief.

"You saved me," Etta whispered.

Gideon's hand rose to brush a thumb over her cheek. "You saved Westrende."

"It doesn't feel like it."

"It will, in time. We can make certain it's so."

Then he leaned in to kiss her right there in the council chamber, though the others were so deep into planning they would probably never know. Etta didn't bother looking. She closed her eyes, wrapping her arms around him and feeling as if she might be willing to lie right there on the council floor and take a nap, at least as soon as she'd had enough of

Gideon's soft, sweet kisses. He pulled her more deeply into the embrace, pressing his lips into her hair and the base of her ear, to every part of her he touched.

"We should get Nickolas out of his cell," Etta murmured.

Gideon's attentions trailed the line of her jaw until his lips found hers once more.

Etta drew back to ask, "Did you hear me? About Nickolas."

Gideon leaned in to kiss her again. She gave him a look.

"Very well." He took hold of her hand, as if he could not bear to lose contact. "Let us cease this perfectly enjoyable moment that we've both earned dearly to go let the poor cockscomb out of his cell."

Etta let out a helpless laugh. "Thank you for mustering the enthusiasm. I do owe him. It's the least I can do not to leave him locked in a dungeon." She hesitated, glancing back at the council. "Is there not something you need to see to? I'm sure I can manage a jailbreak with just a note from the chancellor, not the chancellor himself."

Gideon shrugged. "I have a clerk to dismiss and a few other concerns to clear up. But it can wait. The rest of this day belongs to you, my lady. If you want to spend it on Lord Brigham—"

Etta gave him a quick elbow to the ribs, smiling as they turned to walk from the room. "Lord Alexander, I was entirely wrong about you."

"Is that so?" he asked.

"Yes. It's going to be a great deal more fun to keep the lord chancellor in check than I anticipated."

EPILOGUE

A week later

"My lady," Gideon murmured, his body only inches from hers while his dark eyes trailed every line of her face. "I fear the worst has happened."

"Has it?" Etta replied.

Gideon hummed gravely in affirmation. "It seems I've become infatuated." He shook his head as his gaze fell to trace her lips. "I may not be able to comport myself."

"This is perhaps not a crime you should be confessing to a law official."

He leaned closer. "Precisely why I thought it best to get it off my chest. Before it's too late."

Etta grabbed hold of his uniform and jerked him near, planting a kiss on his lips as her free hand toyed with the freshly cut hair at the nape of his neck. After a long moment, she drew away to look at him. "Better?"

"Much," he said in a low, rough voice before he leaned in to kiss her again.

"Oh, truly," a sullen voice said from down the hall.

Gideon paused but did not look away.

"Well, well, well. Lord Alexander, look who's unbecoming now. Cavorting in a public corridor with an official of Westrende, the both of you." Nickolas clicked his tongue, his hand waving in some gesture that was probably supposed to imply disappointment.

Etta didn't bother looking away, either, even as Gideon replied, "It's not a public corridor. I cannot fathom how you gained access."

"I have connections." When they still didn't give him their full attention, Nickolas crossed his arms. "I see where I rate now." Gesturing over a shoulder, he asked, "Shall I just tell them you're not coming? That you'd rather stand here and gaze longingly into each other's eyes?"

Etta did look at him then. "You know I'll be able to arrest you by the time this ceremony is over."

"It wouldn't be the first time you've had me thrown in jail." He threw a glance at Gideon then pointed a finger toward his own collar, where Gideon's was out of place. He bit back a smile as the chancellor rushed to put himself into order. "Lady Ostwind," Nickolas said, "I meant to offer to walk you, but I see now that you have someone already fit for your arm. I suppose this means I'll be stuck escorting my mother. Thanks for that. Nothing like being abandoned for a stodgy officer of the court." When Gideon glared up at him, Nickolas shot Etta a wink. "I'll meet you later."

As he turned to go, he glanced back over his shoulder. "I was wrong, by the way. That color suits you perfectly."

Etta tried very hard to wipe the smile from her face as she straightened the sword at her hip, tugged down the hem of her marshal's coat, and took Gideon's proffered arm.

They came into a corridor filled with courtiers, men and women who served Westrende, and not a single one of them fae. Her mother, head of council and by unanimous vote the new General Ostwind, had been swift in her removal of the shadows, and the revelation had scattered many of the lesser fae. Etta had never felt safer, more proud, or more certain that her mother's vows would all be done. She'd sworn to win back the general, and with any luck, it would be done before the next moon. They would be a family again.

"I've a council member to speak to." Gideon's voice was low, sending a shiver through her as it brushed her bare neck. He was right—they were in trouble. "Infatuation" was not a strong enough word. "I'll return to you in a moment."

She nodded then walked the line of portraits to where the final one hung. A new artist had been called to paint over the work the fae had done, the canvas patched, and a plate installed that read Antonetta's full name. Beneath it, engraved in metal: Marshal of Westrende.

Etta came to stand beside Jules, who stared up at it. "It's truly lovely, my lady. Congratulations on gaining the post."

Etta smiled toward the canvas. Jules would not have any idea that Etta had been Margaretta. Gideon had told the chancery staff that their newest assistant had returned home to care for family. Without the glamour, Etta would not be able to thank Jules for all that she had done. Still, she said, "Thank you. I'm grateful for the help I received to get here."

Jules shook her head. "I cannot believe you let them paint over it. But I suppose it's safer on this wall than anywhere else."

Etta's face snapped to look at her. "Do you mean... as evidence in the Lord Barrett crime?"

Jules laughed. "No, my lady, not that. You were right, though. The original was hideous. The swan alone."

Something brushed Etta's arm, and she turned from her

gaping to find Gideon, his brow drawn in obvious concern. "Is something amiss?"

Etta looked back to Jules, but the woman was gone. Etta scanned the crowd for any sign of her.

"They're waiting on you," Gideon urged.

Etta shook herself, and when she turned toward Gideon, he was watching her as if to see if all was well. He had said before that Jules was protected. Etta would ask him later what that meant and what he knew of Jules. She nodded, inhaled deeply, then took his arm.

They walked the length of the corridor, courtiers moving from their path, the mood of the hall buoyant. He led her to the dais, where upon the platform, a dozen council members waited. In a matter of moments, Etta would be awarded the band that marked her a Westrende official. She was steps away from becoming marshal.

Beside her, Gideon leaned in. "Ready?"

Etta glanced up at the waiting figures atop the dais with a smile. "Lord Chancellor, you should know by now. An Ostwind is always ready."

Discover more in the Rivenwilde world with Nickolas's story (and Jules!), *Within the Hollow Heart*

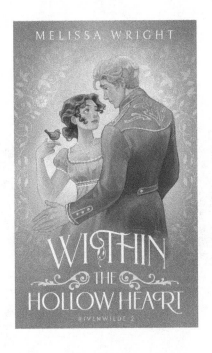

A Rivenwilde Standalone

ALSO BY MELISSA WRIGHT

Shifting Fate

Reign of Shadows

SHATTERED REALMS

King of Ash and Bone

Queen of Iron and Blood

- WITCHY PNR -

HAVENWOOD FALLS

Toil and Trouble

BAD MEDICINE

Blood & Brute & Ginger Root

Visit the author on the web at

www.melissa-wright.com